ONE
MAN
GUY

ONE MAN GUY

Michael Barakiva

FARRAR STRAUS GIROUX
NEW YORK

macteenbooks.com

Library of Congress Cataloging-in-Publication Data

Barakiva, Michael.
    One man guy / Michael Barakiva. — First edition.
        pages cm
    Summary: "When Alek's high-achieving Armenian-American
parents send him to summer school, he thinks his summer is ruined.
But then he meets Ethan, who opens his world in a series of truly
unexpected ways"—Provided by publisher.
    ISBN 978-0-374-35645-3 (hardcover)
    ISBN 978-0-374-35646-0 (ebook)
    [1. Gays—Fiction.   2. Coming out (Sexual orientation)—Fiction.
3. Love—Fiction.   4. Armenian Americans—Fiction.]   I. Title.

PZ7.B229538On 2014
[Fic]—dc23

2013033518

Farrar Straus Giroux Books for Young Readers may be purchased
for business or promotional use. For information on bulk purchases
please contact Macmillan Corporate and Premium Sales Department
at (800) 221-7945 x5442 or by e-mail at specialmarkets@macmillan.com.

To Rafael
When I started this book
I didn't realize
I was writing it for you

And,

To my family
For providing endless love, support, and,
Of course,
Material

"*One belongs to New York instantly. One belongs to it as much in five minutes as in five years.*"
—Tom Wolfe

"*If you can make a good bargain with an Armenian, you can make a good bargain with the devil.*"
—Ancient Persian saying

"*I got the outfit for the party.*"
—Rufus Wainwright, "Rashida"

ONE
MAN
GUY

1

ALEK STARED AT THE MENU SUSPICIOUSLY. HE SMELLED
marinara sauce and a trap.

"Welcome to Trattoria dell'Arte. My name is Lizzy. Can I
start you off with something to drink?" The waitress was young,
maybe a college student already home for the summer, with a
kind, round face framed by bangs that curled up at the bottom.
Alek pitied her. She had no idea what she was in for.

"What bottled water do you have?" Alek's mother asked, while
his father and brother inspected the menu like enemy drones
searching for their opponents' weak spots. Even though both of
his parents were born in this country, Alek's mom spoke with the
slight accent she inherited from the Little Armenia neighborhood
in Los Angeles where she grew up. Most of the time the accent
just hovered in the background of her speech, elongating her vow-
els and giving her an untraceable European mystique. But when

she needed to, like now, she turned it on the way a spider might weave an especially enticing web to lure its prey in for the kill.

"Bottled water, coming right up!" Lizzy responded cheerfully, misunderstanding.

"No, we'd like to know the *brand* of the bottled water," Alek's father specified.

"Oh," Lizzy said, as if he might be kidding.

"You see, many bottled waters actually have levels of contaminants equal to or even higher than tap." Alek's mom informed poor Lizzy of this information as if doing her a favor.

Alek looked at his older brother, Nik, but he continued ignoring Alek. Alek turned back to Lizzy pityingly, futilely trying to telepathically prepare her for the ordeal about to transpire.

"We have Evian," Lizzy offered.

"Evian's good," his father agreed.

Lizzy relaxed. "So, Evian to start?"

"Do you keep any at room temperature?" Alek's mother asked.

"Excuse me?" Lizzy asked nervously. Alek suspected the full horror of the situation was slowly dawning on her.

Alek's mom seized the opportunity to educate. "Digesting chilled water actually taxes the body," she lectured, "because the body has to bring anything it ingests up to its own temperature before it reaches the stomach. That's why we prefer room temperature water."

"It's easier on the system," Nik added, as if this was something everyone should know.

"I can ask," Lizzy offered weakly, succumbing to the three-person tag team.

4

"That would be great," Alek's mother continued. "And if not, would you ask someone in the kitchen to warm it to room temperature?"

Lizzy laughed, as if Alek's mother was making a joke. But Alek knew she wasn't.

"Not more than sixty-eight degrees, please. Seventy at most," she instructed. "I don't want it to be *warm*, because then we'd have to put ice in it, and that would just be adding contaminants, which would defeat the whole point. I'm sure you understand." Alek suspected Lizzy was wondering what heinous crime she had committed in a previous life to get stuck with this table. "Unless, of course, you have ice made from bottled water."

"No," Lizzy said slowly, as if she were talking to a dangerous criminal. "I think all of our ice is from tap."

"So let's see if we can find some Evian at room temperature," Alek's mother concluded. Lizzy scuttled off.

Alek thought it should be illegal for Armenians to go to restaurants. Or that at least they should come with a warning like cigarettes: "Waiting on Armenians Might Be Hazardous to Your Health." The problem was that Armenians prided themselves on being such good cooks that they resented paying money for something they felt they could do better.

"I wish they had zatar here." Nik pitched his voice just loud enough that the staff could hear him complain about the absence of the Middle Eastern spice mixture.

"We can make some when we get home," his mother said. Alek wondered if non-Armenian families spent their time at restaurants planning backup meals when the institutions they were patronizing inevitably disappointed them.

"So, Alek, your mother and I have to talk to you about something," his father began.

"I know," Alek responded. "And I know it must be bad since I've been begging you to bring me here for months." He dunked a piece of bread into olive oil.

"You know, they might just be doing something nice," Nik said. Alek could hear the implied *Not like you deserve it* trailing off his brother's words.

"Well, spit it out and let's get it over with," Alek said.

"You're going to summer school!" his mother announced, as if he'd just won a prize.

"I'm what?" Alek abandoned the glistening piece of bread on his plate.

"They said you're going to *summer school,*" Nik repeated from across the table.

"It's not that I couldn't hear them, dimwit. It's just that I didn't believe it," Alek snapped.

"Aleksander, please lower your voice," his father admonished him, absentmindedly running his hands over the salt-and-pepper beard he'd grown this year. "We're in public."

If Alek had been in a better mood, he might've made a joke about Armenians' deluded belief that, like royalty, paparazzi tracked their every action. But he wasn't. "Why'm I going to summer school? It's not like I failed or anything." Alek's mind began racing, trying to figure out what miracle he could perform in the last week of school that might alter this terrible fate.

"Honey, Ms. Schmidt said she'd be willing to make an exception for you," Alek's mom explained. "She said that if you retook English and math and earned high enough grades, you could stay on Honor Track next year."

"You spoke to Ms. Schmidt behind my back? This is a total conspiracy."

"Aleksander, you are fourteen years old. We are your parents. When we speak to your guidance counselor, it's for your own good," his father scolded him.

"Well, maybe I can still get my grades up—"

Alek's mother cut him off. "Ms. Schmidt told us that even if you got the highest scores possible, it still wouldn't keep you on Honor Track."

"Well, who cares about that?" Alek fought back. "I'll just take Standard next year. It's not like that would be the end of the world."

"You know, Alek," his father started, "South Windsor has one of the best public school systems in New Jersey. Your great grandparents fled Turkey during the genocide of the Armenian people almost one hundred years ago and ended up in this country with nothing. They gave up their land, their belongings, and their history to come to a country where they could be safe and where their children would grow up without persecution and receive the best education in the world."

Alek knew that when his dad starting speaking "Old World," things were bad.

"Their sacrifice means you have a responsibility to do the best you can," his father concluded.

"But what about tennis camp?" Alek cried out.

His parents spotted Lizzy returning with a bottle of Evian

and stopped talking immediately. *God forbid an outsider be privy to the secrets of the Family Khederian*, Alek thought.

"I have good news—we keep some Evian at room temperature in storage," Lizzy said, naïvely opening the bottle.

"I wish you had mentioned that they were plastic bottles," Alek's mother lamented semi-apologetically before Lizzy could pour.

"What?" Lizzy asked.

"We don't drink from plastic," Alek's mother explained, as if the words coming out of her mouth made perfect sense. "First of all, polyvinyl chloride distributes pollutants that are suspected to disrupt the hormonal balance. Secondly, bisphenol A has been linked to obesity and abnormal chromosomes. And you don't even want to know what the plastic does to the water if it's been left out in the sun!" Alek truly marveled at his mother's ability to say insane things reasonably. "We'll just have some green tea," Alek's mom concluded.

"Can I tell you about the specials?" Lizzy asked, taking a step back in preparation for the anticipated assault.

"Actually, can we ask a few questions first?" Alek's dad countered.

"Sure," Lizzy responded wearily. Alek's parents wound up for the interrogation.

"What farm do you get your mozzarella from?"

"Which of the vegetables are locally sourced?"

"Are the tomatoes organic?"

"Are the pickles boiled before they're brined?"

"Are the peas fresh or frozen?"

"Is the rack of lamb domestic or international?"

Lizzy consulted the notes she'd frantically taken on her little pad. "Um, let me see. The mozzarella is generic, I think some of the squash and cucumbers are local, and I don't know about the tomatoes. What else did you ask? Something about pickles?"

Lizzy did her best as the tag-team barrage continued, but by the time it ended, her spirit had been broken. Nik's not-so-subtle sneers every time she failed to answer a question didn't help.

"Do you know what you'd like to eat?" she asked meekly, holding her notepad like a shield. "Or do you need a little more time?"

"I think we're still deciding," Alek's father said.

Alek swore he heard the formerly kind Lizzy muttering obscenities under her breath as she left. "At least with tea, they'll have to boil the water, so we know it's safe," his mother confided to the table. "Now, what were we saying?"

"I was asking how I can go to summer school when tennis camp starts in two weeks. Remember tennis camp? That thing you *promised* I could do because you wouldn't let me try out for the team this year?"

"We didn't let you try out because we thought that time would be better spent on improving your grades. I'm afraid tennis camp is going to have to wait as well," his father informed him.

"But what about the deposit? You know they're not going to give that back," Alek pointed out.

"We know, Alek," his mother responded. "But it's a loss we're willing to bear. Academics come first in our house."

"This sucks," Alek hissed.

"Don't use that word," his father said reflexively. Alek remembered the first time he heard one of his friends curse in front of his parents—a real curse, not *damn* or *suck*. That would never fly in his home.

"Well, if you find the work too challenging, I'd be happy to help you with it." Nik smirked.

Alek kicked his brother under the table.

"Alek, stop that!" his mom reprimanded him. "People will talk!" She looked around to see if anyone had witnessed the inexcusable faux pas.

"God, Mom, don't you understand, nobody is looking at us. Nobody cares what we do. I can stand on top of this table and throw bread at him and they wouldn't care." To demonstrate his point, Alek picked up the piece of now-soggy bread, drenched in oil and balsamic vinegar, and aimed it across the table at Nik.

"Aleksander, that's enough," his father scolded him. "Now put that bread down, sit at this table like an adult, which is how you're always asking to be treated, and enjoy the meal we're paying for."

The meal Mom's paying for, Alek thought to himself. But he knew better than to say that out loud. Ever since his dad got laid off from his architectural firm last year and his mom had to return to work full-time, Alek's dad had been especially sensitive to the money issue.

"Well, thanks, guys," Alek said, the saccharin pouring off his voice. "Let's see—you think I'm an idiot, you tell me one week before school ends that I'm going to have to spend the rest of my summer in the den of despair that is my high school, I can't go to tennis camp even though you *promised* I could—is there anything else you want to lay on me?"

"Well," Alek's mom said, fidgeting with her napkin.

"Oh my God, are you kidding me? What else can there possibly be?"

His mom looked at his dad for help, but he was scrutinizing the menu as if it were the Ark of the Covenant.

"You don't have to be in the top five percent of your class like I am to figure it out," Nik observed. "If you're doing summer school, you're not going to be able to go on the family vacation."

"Now, Andranik, we'll handle this," his father said, finally looking up. Nik, who'd sprouted another four inches his junior year, had the decency to shut up for once. "You see, Alek, when we committed to going to Niagara Falls with the other families from church this summer, we bought into a group deal. If we pulled out now, we'd jeopardize everyone else's vacation."

"Not to mention that I had to ask special permission to get those days off from camp," Nik added.

"You're telling me that you're choosing the people from church over your own son for our *family* vacation?" Alek asked incredulously. "And I'm sure the fact that Nik's girlfriend is one of those people is a total coincidence, right? I mean, I'm used to you choosing Nik over me, but choosing Nanar over your own flesh and blood? That's a new all-time low."

"She has nothing to do with it," Nik interjected.

"Whatever."

"Alek, Nanar's family is just one of the many families we'd be letting down if we backed out now," his mother explained.

Nik flipped through the menu, the disdain with which he turned the pages making it clear he wasn't impressed. "Besides, all of us from Armenian Youth are planning on researching our heritage projects in the Toronto Archives."

"Not to mention losing all of our money," his father concluded.

"I still don't understand why we didn't just take a normal family vacation by ourselves," Alek asked petulantly.

"Well, if that's what you want to do next year, that's what we'll do. Your father and I decided that because you can't go this year, you'll get to choose where we go next summer."

"If I don't have to go back to summer school, you mean," Alek rifled back. "Because who knows? Maybe I'll get another"—he gasped for dramatic effect—"God forbid—another C, and they'll threaten to kick me off Honor Track again, and I'll have to sacrifice another summer of my life to the cruelest institution in the history of mankind."

"Be reasonable . . ." his father began, but stopped when he saw Lizzy walking back slowly, balancing a pot of hot water and four mugs with tea bags in them.

Alek's mother smiled at the waitress when she reached the table. Lizzy took it as a good sign, but Alek knew better. "Do you have any loose tea?" his mother asked.

"Loose tea?" Lizzy asked meekly.

"It's just that some studies show that the paper in tea bags—"

"Oh my God!" Alek exploded. "Why are you torturing this poor girl? She's not even related to you! And nobody gets cancer from drinking tea in bags. Do you hear me? NO ONE. And no one gets cancer from drinking Evian in plastic bottles!" The way the other customers in the restaurant were looking at Alek told him he was probably using his outside voice, but he didn't care.

"This is supposed to be my meal? My consolation prize for being betrayed by my parents to a summer of hell? Then we're going to do it my way." He looked at Lizzy, whose befuddlement was quickly morphing into gratitude. "The tea is great, thank you." Alek slammed the menu shut. "I'll have the pasta carbonara. They'll split the grilled steak. And that jerk with his mouth gaping open like a fish in the corner will have the lasagna. And make sure the meat is well-done, okay?"

Lizzy nodded yes, furiously scribbling into her little pad.

"Now quickly, go before they have a chance to say anything!"

Lizzy didn't need any further encouragement. She sprinted away, her apron strings flopping behind her.

The moment Lizzy was out of earshot, Alek's mom leaned in. "I do hope they cook the meat all the way through," she confided. "Otherwise I'll simply have to send it back."

2

"GOODBYE, YOU HELLACIOUS DEN OF SIN!" BECKY screamed at the top of her lungs. She had just popped on her right Rollerblade and was struggling with the left. A few of the kids walking by her locker laughed, but most were in too much of a rush to escape the last day of school to pay her any attention.

"Are you done?" Alek asked miserably.

"Goodbye, you heinous concrete monstrosity!" Becky continued, ignoring him. "Goodbye, you culinary atrocities that parade as lunch! And you barely conscious teachers, a very special goodbye to you!" Becky turned around lopsidedly, still wearing just one skate, and looked through the window at the yard in front of the school, where even the buses lined up looked impatient. She called out to the students outside, knowing they couldn't hear her. "And most importantly, goodbye to you, lemming peers of mine." Becky waved to them vigorously. Some of the students, misinterpreting her, waved back, inspiring Becky to continue. "For three blessed months, my life will be free of you all." Becky had gotten her second skate on and began circling the halls joyfully. "No more meaningless homework assignments and school assemblies. No more—"

"Becky, that's enough," Alek cut her off. He ran his fingers through his thick curly Armenian hair and adjusted the hunter-green JanSport book bag he'd prayed would fall apart every day since his mom gave it to him the first day of seventh grade. "Can we get going, please?"

"Well, somebody's underwear is all knotted up today. Just because you have to go to summer school doesn't mean I should forgo my last-day-of-school ritual."

"I'm just saying, a little bit of consideration wouldn't kill you. I'm still going to have to deal with all the stupid things you're saying goodbye to."

"It's not my fault you're stupid."

"It's not my fault you're a bitch," Alek shot back. He looked down the school corridors, not believing that only six days had passed since his parents had informed him he'd be denied the well-earned summer respite that was every teenager's sacred right. "By the way, 1999 called. They want their Rollerblades back."

"Should I hand over your entire wardrobe while I'm at it?" she asked, one-upping him as usual. "I still don't get why you're even doing it."

"I told you, my parents are making me! Ms. Schmidt told them that if I get A's in algebra and English, I can stay on Honor Track, and then I might even be able to get on AP by junior year."

"Ms. Schmidt is a cow. How can we be expected to take advice from someone who decided to become a guidance counselor? That's like asking a blind man to help you pick a pair of glasses." Becky finally snapped on her last safety pad. "Are you ready? I've been waiting for you for, like, forever."

Alek rolled his eyes.

"Catch me if you can, slowpoke." Becky kicked off and skated down the main hall, where green-and-white athletic banners from past years hung like sloths. A hall monitor halfheartedly called after her, "No rollerblading in the hallways," but Becky ignored the reprimand and flew out the main entrance onto Western Avenue. Alek didn't bother running after her. He knew she'd come back eventually.

Alek made his way up the small hill in front of his high school, trying to figure out why his freshman year had been so miserable. He even missed middle school, he was embarrassed to admit. He might not have been the most popular kid in eighth grade, but he made honor roll without trying, played first doubles for the tennis team, never had to worry about finding a partner for class projects, and had been invited to enough birthday parties and bar/bat mitzvahs to keep himself busy on the weekends.

High school, however, was its own world with its own rules, as Alek was still figuring out. As his grades started slipping, his freshman year fast-forwarded into a blur of conferences and parent-teacher meetings, none of which made any difference. And the harder he tried, the worse he did, like medicine that just made you sicker.

And when Alek's parents didn't let him try out for the tennis team, they effectively cut him off from all his old middle school friends, like Jason and Matthew. Alek's social life hit a new low in humiliation when his mother reached out to some of those kids and invited them over for a surprise birthday dinner party. Alek could tell they only showed up because their parents made them, and that they'd all have rather been at the movies or playing video games. And instead of ordering in pizza, which is what he would've wanted if they'd bothered asking him, his parents insisted on making an entire Armenian feast. What grownups didn't realize was that nothing was more embarrassing than when they tried to help.

The Khederians lived close enough that Alek could walk to and from school when the weather was good, and he and Becky made a point of doing it together. Whenever she didn't have to stay after for band practice, they met in front of her locker after eighth period. Then she'd wheel ahead, eventually circling back up with him just past the tennis courts and the large black ash tree that got hit by lightning last spring.

The sound of a sharp whistle penetrated Alek's brain. He squinted up into the afternoon June sun. "Pay attention, young man," an elderly crossing guard reprimanded him, the folds of wrinkles on her forehead arching in concern. Alek looked up, startled, and stepped back onto the curb, mumbling thanks. He caught a glimpse of Becky up ahead, weaving her way through pedestrians on the sidewalk.

Alek just wasn't one of those people who thrived under pressure, like his old doubles partner. Seth wasn't a better tennis player than Alek, but when it really mattered, Seth would deliver, serving an ace or slamming the forehand winner down the line.

But when Alek felt pressured, time sped up and out of his

control, like when he and Seth had played in the final match last year against Steinbrook. The two teams had been evenly matched, reaching a tiebreaker in the fifth set. Alek and Seth were down five to six on Alek's serve. They needed to win the point to stay in the match.

Seth had trotted over to Alek after he faulted on his first serve. "I'm counting on you, man. You can do it." Seth gave Alek an encouraging pat on the shoulder and resumed his position on the court.

Faulting again would lose them the point and the match, so Alek prepared for his simple-but-reliable second serve. As he planted his feet and prepared to throw the ball in the air, Alek had decided to give the serve everything he had. He hoped the unexpected force would surprise the opposing team. Besides, this was the last match that he would be playing as an eighth grader, and he wanted to make it count. Alek aimed at the corner of his opponents' advantage court, threw the tennis ball high in the air, arched his back, and swung his racket up and around to hit the ball with maximum strength, hoping with every part of himself that the serve would find its mark.

Instead, the ball had slammed meaninglessly into the net. Alek had double-faulted, losing the point and the match.

In the locker room afterward, Seth tried to pull Alek out of the black hole he'd sunk into. "Don't worry about it, dude. It's just tennis."

Alek had looked up, his shoulders relaxing for the first time since his faulty serve. He thought about how much he would miss his tennis partner next year, since Seth would be going to the fancy private high school two townships over. Even though they hadn't really known each other until they started playing together and they didn't have the same friends or hang out together, their tennis partnership had blossomed into its own special type of friendship.

"Hold on to this." Seth held a tennis ball out to Alek.

"Why?"

"It's the ball from your last serve."

"So?"

"I had to get it out from the net. You hit the ball so hard that it got stuck. That's not an easy thing to do, man. If your serve had landed, you would have aced them, no question." Seth leaned forward, and the light caught the gold of the Star of David necklace he had started wearing after his bar mitzvah.

"But I didn't. I double-faulted and lost us the match."

"Come on, man. I'd much rather play with someone who gives it everything he's got than someone who takes the safe route, okay? That's what made playing with you so fun this year."

Alek had stretched out his hand to accept the ball from Seth, and their fingers brushed. Alek kept his hand there, their hands holding the ball in midair between them. Their fingers had remained linked, connecting them and embracing the suspended ball.

Alek thought he saw Seth leaning in right before they both heard the locker room door swing open.

"Aleksander, are you ready?" Alek's father shouted in.

"Yeah, Dad—one sec!" Alek had grabbed the rest of his things and scrambled out. "Hey, Seth . . ." He wanted to thank Seth for having been such a great partner and friend, for being kind to him when most partners would've ripped him apart, but he didn't know how to do any of that without sounding stupid or corny. "Thanks for the ball," he finished, looking away.

"No prob, man."

Alek hadn't seen Seth since then. He thought about reaching out to him, but never actually did because he didn't know what to say. All Alek knew was that he missed Seth differently from everything else in the world he left behind.

3

ALEK TURNED ON ETRA AND SAW BECKY LEANING
against a stop sign.

"What took you so long? I could've taken the SATs waiting
for you."

Even on her skates, Becky barely broke five feet. Nothing
about her appearance, from her frizzy brown hair to her daily
outfit of overalls and a sweater, betrayed her real personality.
Becky had gone to the other middle school in South Windsor,
so Alek hadn't met her until they sat next to each other in Earth
Science on the first day of freshman year. Becky began whispering
asides to Alek about their teacher's ear hair less than five minutes
later, and by the time the bell rang Mr. Cenci had reprimanded
Alek twice for disrupting the class with his laughter. Each time,
Becky stared straight ahead, serious and solemn, feigning inno-
cence at Alek's disruptive behavior.

"So when are you leaving for Maine?" Alek asked.

"Change of plans."

"What happened?"

"I decided to dis my grandma when I found this." She unzipped her book bag and handed Alek a brochure.

"You want to go to skating camp? Really?" Alek flipped through the glossy images of teens performing stunts and tricks.

"It's the last two weeks before school starts. You get to train with pros. I can't wait!" Becky said, spinning with joy. "My folks told me I'd have to pay for it if I wanted to go, so I got a job at Dairy Queen."

"God, I'm so happy that you're going to be here," Alek admitted.

"Everybody's been saying that to me. A few minutes ago, a group of cheerleaders stopped and thanked me for deciding to stay. They said the summer just wouldn't be the same without me."

"It wouldn't! You wanna hit the movies this weekend?"

"Okay, but there's an Audrey Hepburn film that I want to see, too. Why don't we catch whatever mindless-superhero-blockbuster ridiculousness you want on Friday night, and then we can spend a civilized afternoon watching *My Fair Lady* on Saturday? I'll see if Mandy and Suzie can come."

"Do you have to?" Alek asked.

"It might be my last chance to see them before band camp," Becky protested.

"You know I don't like hanging out with girls," Alek said.

"Thanks a lot."

"You know what I mean, Becky. You're not like them. You're different."

"Well, don't even think of standing me up," Becky warned him. "Because if you do, I'll cut you. I've got a reputation around these parts for being a badass. Why do you think no one picks on us? They know you're running with me and my posse."

It was hard to imagine someone less intimidating than Becky. Luckily, South Windsor wasn't the kind of high school where anyone got beaten up. The kids here were interested in getting good grades, getting better SAT scores, and getting into the best colleges. Honor Society students at South Windsor High were treated the way jocks would be at a different school.

"If I'm lucky, this book about the making of *My Fair Lady* will have arrived by then. That's the reason I want to see it again! In fact, I'll probably want to watch it again *after* I read the book, too, so I can really appreciate the nuances."

Alek and Becky continued until they reached Orchard Street.

"I can go down the rest of the way by myself." Becky smiled, initiating their ritual.

"Why don't I walk you to your door?" Alek recited on cue.

The first time Alek and Becky had walked home from school together, he had insisted on taking her all the way to the front door, because "that's what my mother told me a gentleman would do." Becky was so flabbergasted by Alek's bizarre chivalric formality that she let him accompany her. Ever since then, when they arrived at this intersection, they reenacted the exchange.

Alek dropped Becky off, retraced his steps back to Mercer, and continued walking home. A few minutes later, he reached the train station, the halfway point between his house and Becky's.

He heard a train approaching, so he ran to the station to watch it pull in. Alex had fallen in love with a hand-carved wooden miniature locomotive he had received for his second birthday and loved trains ever since. Their strength and speed exhilarated him, especially the express trains that skipped South Windsor, shooting through the station at maximum velocity as if it wouldn't even occur to them to stop at the insignificant suburb. The train pulling in now was a southbound local, originating in New York and traveling into New Jersey. The other side of the station, which Alek had never visited, was for the northbound trains en route to the city.

Over the last few years, Alek had gone into New York with his parents a handful of times. Usually, his family would drive in on a Saturday morning, catch a Broadway matinee or a museum exhibit, and then drive back. Alek begged to stay longer, but Manhattan restaurants made his parents feel claustrophobic, and they flat out rejected Alek's suggestion that they "just walk around for a while." Alek could sense other parts of the city calling to him, neighborhoods hiding behind skyscrapers like exotic animals in a jungle. But these family outings were the only way he could get into the city, and he took what he could get.

The train pulled in and the doors slid open. A few people trickled out, unlike the throngs that got off at the end of the workday. Alek envied them for getting to go to New York, but also pitied them for having to come back to suburbia. It made him think of Tantalus, the character in Ancient Greek mythology he learned about in sixth grade, doomed to thirst and starve in the underworld, with water and food always just out of his reach. Alek didn't know which was worse, being so close to the thing you wanted and not being able to grasp it, like Tantalus, or being exiled from it entirely.

24

The doors closed and the train started to pull away. Alek watched it shoot into the distance, an arrow happily speeding toward its target.

Alek had lived his entire life in the neighborhood on this side of the station. The proud houses stood behind their manicured lawns in perfect lines, and since the housing association insisted they all be painted in the same palette of heinous pastels, the blocks looked like rows of oversize dinner mints in a giant's candy box.

The other side of the station, the New York–bound side, bordered a less welcoming part of town. Because it was South Windsor, it wasn't really dangerous, at least not compared with the parts of New York Alek's parents had described living in before they got married. But the northbound side didn't have the cookie-cutter, squeaky-clean feeling of Alek's.

The two sides of the station had only been connected by a small underground tunnel until an overpass had been built a few years ago. Passing the station every day on his walks to and from school this past year, Alek had fantasized about going to the other side, jumping on a train, and shooting into the city. But Alek's parents had made it abundantly clear that under no circumstances was he allowed to go in without them.

"I know you love New York," Alek's mom told him last month in the car on the way back from their Armenian church. "But the city is very dangerous, especially for someone young. Maybe when you're a senior in high school, and we've had time to explore it together, we'll let you go in. During the day. To a few neighborhoods we would agree on beforehand. With some friends. And a chaperone. And maybe a police escort."

Alek hoped to get some support from his father. "Didn't you move to New York for college when you were just a few years older than I am now?" he asked. But his father wouldn't budge.

"Listen to your mother. The city's not safe."

Alek stood in the opening to the tunnel, peering down. Even in the middle of the day, the tunnel was dim, lit only by sporadically flickering orange fluorescents that made it feel like the setting for a horror movie. Since the overpass had been built, the tunnel had gone mostly unused, forgotten like an old pair of jeans. Although he knew his dad expected him to come home right after school, Alek lingered. The corrugated steel forming the tunnel's opening invited and threatened him at the same time. He took a step in. And then another.

Alek held up his hand and marveled at how the orange light made his flesh look alien. He walked forward, matching his footsteps to the *drip-drip-drip* of a leaky pipe. He focused on the small landscape of sunlight at the end, beckoning him. The air was cooler in the tunnel. Alek inhaled and continued walking.

He emerged in an abandoned parking lot on the northbound side of the station. A bunch of older kids whom he recognized from school were skateboarding on an obstacle course of ramps and traffic pins they had erected. These kids were Nik's age, but Alek knew they weren't part of Nik's Honor Society clique. They were called the Dropouts, or D.O.s for short, because of their impressively challenged graduation rate. Each clique at South Windsor High had its part to play, and you could always count on the Dropouts to sneak cigarettes, cut class, or start fights. Alek didn't know most of them by name, but he recognized the one named Ethan as the initiator of the infamous food fight in March.

Principal Saunder had implemented a dress code that prohibited baggy pants and had just rejected the student petition to have them reinstated. So, the rumors went, Ethan took it upon himself to initiate a cafeteria-wide food fight in protest. Alek didn't share the same lunch period with Ethan, so he hadn't witnessed the fight itself, but he remembered what all the students looked like when they were being marched out of the cafeteria—their clothes drenched in ketchup and milk, bread and potato chip crumbs and God knows what else, and happier than he'd ever seen a group of kids at South Windsor High. Although Alek was glad he hadn't been caught up in that mess, he also wished that it had happened during his lunch period so he could've witnessed the pandemonium.

But even before that food fight, Alek thought Ethan epitomized cool. Today he was wearing army-green cargo pants with buckles and chains looped through them and a black T-shirt that read DARE TO RESIST DRUGS AND VIOLENCE in blocky red letters. Alek looked down at his own boring khaki shorts and dark blue short-sleeved button-down shirt. Even if his parents had let him shop for his own clothes, he wouldn't know where to find anything other than the same boring Gap fare they had always chosen for him.

Alek watched Ethan navigate his skateboard through the obstacle course with ease, laughing and talking to his friends at the same time. Ethan was a few inches taller than Alek, with wavy sandy hair that fell in his face in a way that made Alek think of surfers. Alek's own hair was dark, thick, and unmanageable, like weeds in a garden. He had tried to grow it out last year, but it only got bigger instead of looking cool. All the kids at church referred to it as an Armenian 'Fro, and his parents told him that one day he'd be lucky to have such thick hair, but Alek envied the way Ethan's hair flopped up and down as he jumped over pins, kicked off stairs, and slid down banisters.

A big D.O., his meaty forearms crossed in front of his chest, spotted Alek and called out, "Hey, kid, you got a problem?"

Alek felt his face grow red. He didn't want to look scared, but all he could do was stutter back. "No, um, I, just was, um . . ."

The guy lumbered up to Alek, wiping his runny nose on his arm. He was wearing a short-sleeved plaid shirt that stretched tight across his ample bulk, and his brown hair was clipped on the sides, so short that Alek could see the flesh of his skull. The top of his hair spiked up in a fauxhawk, making him appear even bigger. Alek couldn't remember his name, but knew that he was supposed to have graduated last year. He approached Alek with the confident swagger of home turf. "Spit it out, dude. I said, you got a problem?"

Before Alek could reply, the guy drew his meaty arms back and gave Alek a sharp shove. The force caught him off guard, and Alek fell to the ground. He cried out, more in surprise than pain. The commotion caught the other guys' attention. They skated over, hoping for some afternoon entertainment. Alek stared up from the ground, faces appearing in his field of vision like enemy spaceships.

Jack. Alek suddenly remembered his attacker's name. Jack.

Jack's face hovered menacingly over Alek. "What's your problem? Why don't you stand up and take it like a man?" Alek tried to move away, but the much bigger kid squatted down, using his knees to pin Alek to the ground. Jack barked the questions again, like an army sergeant.

The smell of onions and mustard slammed into Alek's nostrils. *This is what about-to-get-beat-up feels like,* Alek realized. He just hoped that whatever happened, he would emerge without any visible marks so that his parents wouldn't have a reason to ask any questions. Getting beat up was humiliating. Having to explain it to your parents was worse.

When Alek still didn't reply, Jack lowered his face so it was right up against Alek's. "I said, stand up, son," he screamed.

"Leave him alone, Jack." Alek turned his head to see who had come to his rescue. Ethan rolled over calmly and kicked his skateboard up, revealing a collage of colorful stickers on the bottom. The bright green wheels continued spinning as he held his board in one hand and put the other on Jack's shoulder.

Jack locked eyes with Ethan. "I'm just having some fun, man."

"That's what you call fun? Picking on some kid half your size?" Ethan joked. But when Jack didn't get up, Ethan continued, "But I guess the way you've been eating, finding someone your own size to pick on is pretty much impossible."

"You don't have to take that, Jack!" someone called out from behind Alek.

"Yeah, show him who's who!"

Jack's face slowly turned red as the rest of the guys continued taunting them. "Let's see if you're still talking big when you have my fist in your face, Ethan."

"Your fist and my face are pretty much the same size now, big boy," Ethan cracked. With a grunt, Jack jumped off Alek and rushed Ethan, knocking him to the ground. Alek remained on the ground, forgotten, as the faces staring down at him fled to witness the much more exciting spectacle. Alek heard chants of "Get him, Ethan!" and "Show him who's who, Jack," as well as the occasional smack of fists hitting flesh.

Alek thought about sputtering out a thank-you to Ethan, but he decided against calling any more attention to himself. He scrambled to his feet, turned around, and ran through the tunnel and all the way back home.

4

THE MERCILESS BLARING OF HIS ALARM CLOCK WAS A psychic assault on Alek's brain. He cheated his eyes open a sliver. The red numbers glared 7:17. Alek did the math in his head, desperate for a computation that allowed him one more snooze without being late. But when the numbers refused to cooperate, he had to hurl himself out of bed and onto the floor, letting the impact smash him into consciousness. He lay like that for a moment, wondering what Faustian bargain he could make to get out of having to go to the first day of summer school. But there was no flicker of hope, no appearance of a demonic power. Apparently, no one was interested in his soul.

The five days that had elapsed since the end of the school year proper didn't even seem like a minivacation, especially since the rain made Alek spend most of the weekend cooped up with his family.

"Hurry up if you want breakfast," Alek heard his father scream up from downstairs.

Alek had perfected the art of getting ready in twelve minutes flat. He stumbled into the bathroom, turned the shower on, and, while it was warming up, gathered his notebooks and textbooks. He put them in the beat-up green JanSport, glaring at the impossibly long-lived bag with hatred. Then he lay out his clothes. Usually he tried to look nice for the first day of school. But since this was just a program for delinquents and leftovers, denim shorts and a plain mustard T-shirt would do.

He jumped in the shower, scrubbed himself down, hopped out, and toweled himself and his hair dry. Then he threw his clothes on and went downstairs, the 7:29 on the clock proof of his perfected system.

Nik and his mom were already seated at the kitchen table, dressed and ready to start the day. Nik was wearing his new chunky blue eyeglasses, which Alek knew his brother thought made him look cool, but Alek thought were so pathetically wannabe hipster that it was embarrassing.

Alek's brother had always been lanky, but since he started needing to shave, his body had reached almost comedic proportions. Alek didn't think the way he was dressing helped either. For his first day of orientation as a camp counselor, Nik was wearing shorts that he'd rolled up above the knee and a white-and-blue horizontally striped shirt under a dark blue jacket. And to make it worse, he was wearing a red belt to match his red shoes, as if accessorizing well would make up for his total lack of personality.

"Hi, honey," Alek's mom greeted him. She was dressed for

work impeccably as always, with a skirt that came just below her knees and a wraparound light green jacket over a cream blouse. She put her chirping BlackBerry down and looked up at Alek. "Did you sleep well?"

Alek grunted noncommittally and sat down at the table. He wondered if he'd get in trouble for being late, since normally he'd be responsible for helping to lay out the breakfast that greeted him: a pot of hot tea, a pile of freshly baked scones, apricot and blueberry jam, a basket of pita bread, a platter of freshly cut fruit, a plate of thinly sliced cold cuts and cheeses, and, of course, a bowl of zatar. His Dad usually added extra marjoram to the ground herbal mixture, so that by the time it achieved the pasty consistency perfect for pita dipping, it had even more punch. As always, nothing had been touched until everyone was present. The moment Alek sat down, his brother began digging in.

"What do you want in your omelet?" his father asked. He was standing at the stove, wearing a floral kitchen apron over his pajamas, his graying hair in loose curls around his head.

"Whatever," Alek responded.

His father answered enthusiastically, "Well, I've already put in some tomatoes, spinach, and—how about some cheese?"

"I said *whatever*," Alek repeated.

"Okay then," his father continued with gusto. "Some chanakh."

Alek smiled. His dad knew chanakh's biting saltiness made it Alek's favorite. He tossed a healthy pat of butter into the already-warmed skillet, and beat the cheese into the egg-and-vegetable mixture as the butter melted. At the moment after the butter finished bubbling but before it started to burn, he poured in the egg mixture.

Alek dipped the pita in the zatar, gobbled it up, then spread some jam on a scone.

"What's the matter, Alek? You're barely eating," his mother said.

"Do you know what my friends have for breakfast? Like, a bowl of cereal, and that's it!"

"You know *these Americans*," his mother responded. "They don't know the first thing about food. Remember when"—she barely contained her laughter—"remember when you slept over Jason's house in sixth grade?"

"When you still had friends," Nik whispered, earning an under-the-table kick from Alek.

Alek hoped his father would be too busy making the omelets to hear, but he picked up as if on cue.

"Yes, yes, and Jason's parents said you could make pancakes from scratch with them the next morning!" his father joined in.

"What happened? I don't remember," Nik said, although Alek knew he was just giving their parents the excuse they needed to retell the story.

"Well," Alek's mom continued, "Alek woke up the next day, and down they all went to their kitchen. He was so excited, he could barely contain himself. Until, of course, he saw them take out the Bisquick box of pancake mix." Now she turned from Nik to Alek. "Do you remember what you said?"

"No," Alek deadpanned, wishing the ordeal would end.

"Well, I do, because Jason's mom called us that morning and told us all about it. You said, 'That's not from scratch,' and then you proceeded to go to their cabinets and get the flour and baking powder and sugar and salt and mix the batter yourself. And then

34

when you were done, you said, 'Now, *that's* from scratch.'" His family guffawed at the punch line, although Alek didn't see its irrefutable hilarity. "And when you got home, I had to explain to you that to *these Americans*, using a mix *is* making it from scratch."

Alek's parents threw around that phrase—*these Americans*—whenever they wanted to pass judgment without making it sound like they were passing judgment.

"*These Americans* have a television set in every room."

"*These Americans* think dinnertime is five p.m."

"*These Americans* are obsessed with sports."

And on and on they went.

Whenever Alek tried to call his parents out on it, they insisted the phrase was merely descriptive. But the certain lilt they gave it made it clear that whenever *these Americans* did something, Mr. and Mrs. Khederian did not approve. Alek wondered what would happen if he pointed out that since his parents were born in this country, they were just as American as *these Americans*.

"Well, you know what, Mom? *These Americans* don't think that every time you sit down for a meal, you have to eat so much that you feel like you're going to explode."

"So you're saying you don't want your omelet?" his father asked, taking the skillet off the stove top. The smell of the tomatoes, spinach, and chanakh called out to Alek.

"I didn't say that," Alek conceded.

His father walked over, slid the omelet out of the skillet onto Alek's plate, and sprinkled some sugar on top in the traditional Armenian fashion.

"What do you say?" his mother asked pointedly.

"Thanks," Alek muttered.

"*What* do you say?" his mother repeated.

"Thank you," Alek said properly.

"That's better," his mother said. "And wish your father good luck on his job interview."

"You have an interview today?" Alek asked disbelievingly, looking at his father's pajamas-and-apron outfit.

"It's not until the afternoon," his father replied defensively.

"Wish him luck," Alek's mother repeated.

"*Hachoghootyoon,*" Alek mumbled in Armenian, earning him a grateful look from both his parents that wishing luck in English would never have elicited.

"You psyched about your first day of summer school?" Nik asked his brother in between bouts of shoving food into his beanpole body.

"Yeah, I think it's going to be thrilling," Alek answered sarcastically between his own omelet bites.

"Well, my offer stands. If you find the work too challenging, I'd be happy to help you with it. You know, I did tutor for the Honor Society last year." Nik smiled.

"Nik, if I wanted to puke, I could just stick a finger down my throat."

"Aleksander, don't talk like that at the breakfast table," his mom said.

"But he—"

"I just offered to help him," Nik protested innocently. "By the way, Mom, did you see the article on Peter Balakian in the *New York Times* today?" Every time Nik wanted to distract his parents, he brought up something Armenian, and every time, they fell for it.

"Yes, I did, Nik. It was about his new book." His mom beamed at Nik with pride.

"I can't wait to read it. That's the first thing I'm going to buy with my camp money," Nik said.

"Why don't you just borrow my copy?" their father asked.

"I'd like to have my own so that I can take it with me when I go away to college."

Alek thought he really was going to puke now.

"Mom, do you mind if we leave a little early? I want to make sure I make a good impression on the first day," Nik said.

"Of course not," their mom said. "Now, honey." She turned to look at Alek. "When do you want to go shopping for your summer clothes?" she asked, her thumbs dancing over the BlackBerry keyboard.

"You could just drop me off and let me do it myself," he said.

"Maybe next year, honey," his mother responded, eyes still locked on her BlackBerry screen.

"Saturday, then," Alek said, his shoulders slumping in defeat.

"But you were going to take me and Nanar into New York so we could start working on our heritage project," Nik practically whined.

"Are you sure you don't have time to go during the week?" their mother asked Alek.

"I just don't want to commit to anything before I know exactly what my workload for summer school is going to be," Alek shot back sharply. "Cramming an entire year into a few weeks means

37

an enormous amount of homework, as I'm sure you and Ms. Schmidt discussed. Of course, I understand if taking Nik and his Armenian girlfriend into the city is more important than spending time with me. Nik does get better grades, after all. It must be nice to have one child you can be proud of."

His mom looked up from her BlackBerry, frustration and hurt simmering in her eyes. Alek knew he'd gone too far, but instead of saying anything, she just exhaled sadly.

"I guess it'll have to wait, because I'm helping Nik and Nanar on Saturday, and on Sunday we have church."

"If we went to a normal church, like *these Americans*, we wouldn't have to commute three hours every Sunday," Alek responded.

"We're Armenians, Aleksander," his father interjected. "And so we go to an Armenian church. Period. Now is there anything else you'd like to say to ruin everyone's morning?"

"No, that's all. May I be excused from the table? I'd like to be on time for my first day of summer school so I can make a good impression." Without waiting for a reply, Alek grabbed his hated green JanSport and walked out the door.

Passing the turnoff to Orchard Street on the way to school, Alek remembered how he and Becky had cracked each other up after watching *My Fair Lady* that past weekend.

"Goo' mornin', gov'nah," Becky had said, imitating Eliza's Cockney accent before she transformed into an upper-class lady.

Alek mimicked the professor's proper British accent. " 'By right she should be taken out and hung, for the cold-blooded murder of the English tongue!'"

"'The rain in Spain stays mainly in the plain,'" Becky quoted.

"'By George, she's got it! By George, she's got it!'" Alek exclaimed with glee as the professor did when Eliza was finally able to speak properly.

Alek loved hanging out with Becky because it was easy. They had spent almost every weekend of their freshman year like this. After watching a movie, they'd argue about what they did or didn't like or just horse around. Sometimes, they could just sit in a comfortable silence sipping Diet Dr Pepper.

After descending the little hill in front of his school, Alek saw the front entrance was closed for the renovation of the main lobby, so he walked around to the rear. *We don't even get to use the real entrance,* Alek thought. He wondered if he'd know anyone else.

An impressive assembly of South Windsor High's leftovers filed off the buses like disoriented ants. Some looked barely awake. Others were wearing clothes that must've been hand-me-downs of hand-me-downs. Some kids weren't even carrying book bags. Alek fantasized screaming, "Children of dysfunctional families, unite!" and leading this motley crew in a coup of the school.

The other students weren't the only surreal element of summer school. The whole place felt underpopulated, as if it had been ravaged by a devastating plague. Most of the building was closed off, and the classrooms were being painted, so a chemical stench lingered in the hallways. None of the posters for student activities were up, and even small sounds echoed off the walls. It was like walking through a ghost town. Alek half expected to see tumbleweeds blowing down the corridors.

He suffered through English with Ms. Imbrie, then dragged himself down to the cafeteria. Because there were so few students in summer session, the kitchen was closed and everyone was expected to bring their own lunches. He plopped down at the table where he and Becky usually sat, hoping against reason that she would materialize out of thin air and entertain him the way she did during the regular school year. He even missed her jabs at the Armenian food his parents inevitably packed for him, such as today's dolma, with baklava for dessert and a yogurt drink to wash it all down. Although he was sure that Nik would've shown it off proudly, Alek would've killed for a PB&J, some Lay's potato chips, and a flavorless waxy red apple.

Alek could see the entire cafeteria from the table he'd chosen in the corner. To his dismay, he saw the entire pack of Dropouts enter and claim their usual table in the middle of the room. *Of course they're all here,* he thought. He turned, sitting with his back to the rest of the room, staring into a corner. The only way to make it through the hell of summer school, Alek decided, was to turn himself off to everything, not saying or doing anything, until the entire experience was over. It would be his Zombie Summer.

When the truncated summer school lunch period ended, the students in the cafeteria made their way to their afternoon session. Alek walked to his Algebra classroom in the annex and sat all the way in the back, just like he had done earlier that day, wishing he could camouflage into the wall. A poster of Charlie Brown staring at a stack of books with the words THE MORE I

KNOW THE MORE I KNOW HOW MUCH I STILL DON'T KNOW hung next to the chalkboard. Alek took his algebra book out, opened his notebook, and slumped back in the chair. The bell rang, and the teacher stood up from his desk and closed the door behind him.

Alek had only heard of Mr. Weedin and his reputation for unfailing, by-the-book strictness. A tall, thin man who looked like a bald eagle and wore spectacles on the very bottom of his nose, Mr. Weedin had a haughty way of looking down at everyone. And his British accent only made it worse.

"Welcome to Algebra I and II. Because there were so few algebra summer school students, the school administrators, in their infinite wisdom, have decided to combine the classes. I will spend the first half of the period teaching Algebra I, while the Algebra II students can review their homework from the night before. Then the Algebra I students can get a head start on their homework while I teach the Algebra II lesson for the day. If you have any questions, please don't hesitate to—"

The classroom door swung open, interrupting Mr. Weedin's well-rehearsed lecture.

"How's it going, teach?"

Alek looked up and saw Ethan strut into the classroom. Immediately, Alek sat up straight in his chair.

"Ethan Novick, am I correct?" Mr. Weedin asked, consulting his class roster.

"You got it. Sorry I'm late. I got permission to go off campus for lunch today and I busted a wheel on my board getting back."

"Mr. Novick, your modes of transportation are of no interest to me. If you don't pass this class, you will have to repeat your junior year, and I'm sure you don't want that any more than the teachers here do." Mr. Weedin addressed the entire class. "Because each summer school class is the equivalent of a week of work, anyone who cuts without a proper excuse will fail the term. Period. And three tardies count as one absence." He refocused on Ethan. "So, Mr. Novick, for your sake as well as my own, please be more responsible in the future, because if you're late two more times, you will fail."

"No prob, teach," Ethan replied. He made his way to the back of the classroom. Ethan's lower lip was swollen, Alek noticed, and he wondered if it was a memento from his tussle with Jack on the last day of school. Ethan threw his book bag on the empty seat next to Alek and sat down. Alek looked away quickly. He wanted to thank Ethan for intervening and saving him, but he didn't even know if Ethan remembered him.

"Algebra I students, let's begin with integers. Please turn to the first chapter in your book. Class, please note the seats in which you're sitting—they will be your assigned seats for the rest of the summer," Mr. Weedin said from the front of the classroom.

Alek thought that he'd be able to just tune out and let summer school wash over him. But with Ethan sitting so close, it was hard to concentrate on anything. Alek opened his algebra textbook to the first chapter. He figured out that if he angled his body just so, and tilted his book just the right way, he could make it look like he was reading about integers while enjoying a perfect view of Ethan.

5

"IT'S HERE! IT'S HERE!" BECKY SQUEALED WITH JOY AS SHE attacked the nondescript cardboard package that had arrived at her house earlier that day.

The first week of summer school had finally ended, and Alek was treating himself to an evening at Becky's with movies.

"What is?"

"*The Dinner Party Movie Cookbook*! It's a collection of recipes of food made in famous movies—*Gosford Park*, *Big Night*, *Babette's Feast*, and *Guess Who's Coming to Dinner*! I didn't think it was going to show up until next week." The packaging lay tattered around Becky, who was thumbing through the book affectionately.

"Do you think you spend too much time obsessing over movies?"

"Well, what else am I going to do? Live my life? I'd rather watch attractive, well-dressed people do it for me." Becky ran down the stairs to the basement, where the entertainment system was set up. Alek followed. Becky's parents had only gotten partway through finishing the basement, so half of it still looked like an industrial work space.

"Where are your folks?" Alek asked her.

"Conference. Somewhere in Switzerland, I think?"

"And they left you alone?"

"Sure. I told them that if I'm old enough to babysit, I'm old enough to not need a babysitter. Besides, what'm I going to do? Throw a kegger and invite the woodwind section?"

"Good point."

Most of Becky's other friends, like Mandy and Suzie, were fellow marching band geeks. But when they all decided to go to band camp that summer, Becky had refused to even entertain the notion, because she said it was clichéd. Alek really admired Becky, who, unlike most girls her age, was happy to do her own thing, even if that meant sitting at home watching movies or spending the day skating by herself.

Becky and Alek plopped down on the sectional in the middle of the room, facing the flat screen. "What are we going to watch tonight?" Alek asked.

"*Guess Who's Coming to Dinner*. It has Spencer Tracy and Katharine Hepburn. And, of course, Sidney Poitier."

"So what's this movie about?"

Becky gasped in shock. "Are you being serious?"

"Not all of us are obsessed with old movies, you know."

"I worry about what you would do without me," Becky said. She leaned forward and began to explain the plot as if Alek's life depended on it. "Spencer Tracy and Katharine Hepburn play these really liberal upper-class parents, and their daughter arrives from a vacation with this dashing black doctor played by the super-dreamy Sidney Poitier, and she's like, 'We just met, but we're going to get married.' Now, her parents have raised her to be open-minded and everything, but when they're faced with her actually marrying a man of color, they freak. The movie's about the difference between your beliefs and reality. And, mostly, the importance of a good dinner party."

"So you've seen it before?"

"Of course I have. What do I look like, a loser?"

"Of course not. You know you're the coolest girl at South Windsor High."

Becky flipped her hair back mock-provocatively. "I know, like, all the guys on the football team totally want to ask me out," she upward inflected. "But I'm, like, too busy dating the soccer team to make time for them. Do you think I'm a slut?"

"Um, I don't, but you should read what they write about you in the guys' bathroom. They say you're easy."

"Oh my God! Shut up! No way! This is so humiliating! Every guy I slept with promised he wasn't going to say anything! I mean, this is totally gonna destroy my reputation. And then Daddy isn't going to buy me that two-door BMW convertible with tan leather interior!" Becky squeezed her eyes together and pretended to cry. She dropped the act and turned to Alek. "Can we watch the movie now?"

Two hours later, the end credits rolled on the TV, and Becky plopped her head down on Alek's lap. She had started crying toward the end of the movie, and her trails of tears had transformed into gushers in the last scene, when Spencer Tracy's character gave his speech about the hurdles that an interracial couple would face, but that being in love demanded that they marry anyway.

"It's so beautiful. I just can't get over how beautiful it is," Becky wailed.

"It's okay, it's okay. It's just a movie," Alek said soothingly, running his fingers through her brown hair, noticing it was less frizzy than usual. Becky was the first close friend Alek had who was a girl, and he was surprised at how physically comfortable they had grown with each other in the last year. Becky adjusted her head on Alek's lap, and he continued stroking her hair.

Slowly, Becky stopped crying. She went to the bathroom, blew her nose a few times, washed her face, and returned, her nose and eyes still puffy.

"So how's summer school going? You haven't told me anything."

Alek felt his face flush red. Becky knew how upset he'd been about having to go to summer school, but what she didn't know was now he found himself looking forward to it. Especially Algebra.

"Summer school is stupid and the people there are stupid," Alek covered.

"Alek, why didn't you just take Standard next year? That way, you wouldn't need to spend your summer stuck in that den of despair."

"That's not how it works in my house. There are a bunch of things that come with being Armenian. Like, you only go to the Armenian Orthodox Church, even if it means driving one and a half hours *each way*. And chess and classical music, you have to like both of those things, and you never, ever eat in a Turkish restaurant or buy clothes made in Turkey."

"What's up with the anti-Turkish stuff?" Becky asked. "That sounds pretty racist."

"Do you think it would've been racist for the American Indians to be pissed at European settlers for ravaging their people and stealing their lands?" Alek asked heatedly. "Or for the Jews to have issues with the Nazis who committed the Holocaust?"

"No, but—" Becky retreated.

"Well, that's exactly what the Turks did to the Armenians before and during World War I. And it's not like the Turkish government even admits it. It'd be one thing if they were, like, setting displaced Armenians up in casinos or building memorials or giving our land back. But they pretend that it never happened. 'Casualties of war' is what they claim. But casualties of war are supposed to be from the other side, not the government of the country you live in forcing your people in death marches across the desert."

"Okay, Alek, jeez. I was just asking a question."

Alek slowly released the fists he hadn't realized he'd been clenching. "You know how your parents read you stories when you were a kid?"

"Sure," Becky said.

"Well, this was a bedtime favorite in the Khederian house." He closed his eyes and recited:

> *"Should it happen we do not endure*
> *this uneven fight and drained*

47

of strength and agonized
we fall on death's ground, not to rise
and the great crime ends
with the last Armenian eyes
closing without seeing a victorious day,
let us swear that when we find
God in his paradise offering comfort
to make amends for our pain,
let us swear that we will refuse
saying No, send us to hell again.
We choose hell. You made us know it well.
Keep your paradise for the Turk."

"What is that?" Becky asked.

" 'We Shall Say to God.' It was written by Vahan Tekeyan, this really famous Armenian poet. It's the last lines that really hit me. 'We choose hell. You made us know it well. / Keep your paradise for the Turk.' That's what my parents were reading to me when you were getting Snow White or the Little freakin' Mermaid."

"Well, dude, that's messed up," Becky said.

"Tell me about it. But they couldn't help it. And neither can I. We are all the thing we were raised to be." Until now, Alek thought this Armenian stuff was important to his parents, or to Nik, but not to himself. "How'd we even end up talking about this?"

"You were defending Armenians' blatantly racist policies," Becky reminded him.

"That's right. Well, after the Turkish thing, the next most important thing is doing well at school."

"It all sounds too intense for me. I mean, I got C's in Standard History and Phys Ed last year, and my parents just told me to try harder next time. And that time I cut class to go skating in the park, they were just like, 'Tell us next time so we can write you a note.'"

"That is absolutely and utterly incomprehensible to me. If I cut class, my parents would freak out."

"At least they didn't make you get a summer job."

Alek put his feet up. "Oh, that's right—how're things at DQ?"

"Thought it would be fun. Was totally wrong. My manager, Laurie, is this rhinoceros of a woman. She gets angry when any of the employees' friends visit, but I want to be like, 'At least they're attracting some customers to this pathetic business—what do you care if they hang out and want to talk for a few minutes?' And the rest of the customers—don't even get me started. You know that saying 'When hell freezes over'? That's Dairy Queen."

"Why don't you quit?"

"I told you—I have to make enough to go to skating camp. And I've decided I need a new pair of blades, too—my Activas just aren't going to cut it anymore. Besides, do you know how hard it is for a fourteen-year-old to get any kind of gainful employment? Especially after summer's started and every place has already hired people?"

"Becky, let me ask you a question."

"Shoot."

"Has there ever been something that you've wanted to do but were scared to?"

"I don't know," Becky said, looking confused. "What are you talking about?"

Alek had spent the last week trying to thank Ethan for intervening at the parking lot, but he hadn't figured out how to do it.

"Well, I keep on trying to get my courage up to do something, but every time I bail out at the last minute."

Becky tilted her head and looked at Alek for a few moments. "If you want to do something, then you have to trust your instincts and do it," she said decisively, squinting at him like he was out of focus. She scootched her way next to Alek on the sofa. "Because you never know how something's going to end up."

Alek waited for her to say or do something else, but when that didn't happen, he cleared his throat loudly. But she still just sat there and closed her eyes.

"Becky, it's getting late and I need to start on some homework. I'll see you soon, okay?"

Becky opened her eyes quickly, like she had just woken up. "Soon, okay. No problem. We'll find some time when I'm not serving up Double Fudge Cookie Dough Blizzards."

Alek never woke up early on Saturday mornings. But the next day, he made an exception, because he wanted to show off his first test to his parents. Mr. Weedin had walked up and down the aisles of the classroom the day before, returning the exams to the students. Each time he gave back a test, he'd follow it with a pointed remark, spoken just loud enough so that the entire class could infer how you'd done. For example, when he handed Emily Fink her test back, he said disappointedly, "Emily, I would recommend studying next time. It does wonders." To

Ethan, Mr. Weedin said, "Mediocre at best, Mr. Novick." But when he got to Alek, his face almost eased up. "Well done, Mr. Khederian. Well done, indeed."

Alek held the test with a big fat red circled ninety-three on top, waiting for his parents to wake up. He had wanted to show it to them when he got back from Becky's the night before, but they were already asleep. Two hours of Saturday morning cartoons later, he heard them stirring above. He scampered up the stairs to their bedroom and put his ear to the door to make sure they were actually awake. He hoped that they'd be so impressed with his test that he'd be invited to go into New York with Nik and Nanar, and maybe they'd even drop him off somewhere while they researched their heritage projects.

"Boghos, I just feel like I'm at my wit's end with him."

"It's not like he failed, Kadarine."

"I'm not talking about summer school. I'm talking about all of it. Where is that sweet little boy we brought up? The last year, his behavior's been, well, relentless."

"This has been a hard time for all of us, Kada. With you having to go back to work full-time, and me, well—"

"Honey, I know you'll find another job soon."

"All I mean is that this has been a tough time for everyone, and we'll all come through it. Alek's no exception. Besides, he's a teenager. This is how they behave."

"Nik didn't—"

"Nik hasn't yet. But who knows what he'll be like next year, or when he goes to college?"

"Don't look at me like that, Boghos. We did a good job bringing our sons up. Why did I take years out of my life to raise and spend time with my children if they're going to behave like *these American* kids who were brought up by nannies and babysitters and day care centers?"

Alek couldn't listen anymore. He tiptoed away from the door and to his room, quietly closing his door behind him. He dropped the test into the trash can underneath his desk. He played his mother's words over and over in his head, and each time they stung more.

Alek stayed in his room for the next few hours. His mother had chosen a moss green for the walls and a complementary light oak bedroom set for the furniture. Alek wished the walls were painted in a bolder color, like orange, but he figured that if his mom wasn't letting him buy his own clothes yet, there was no point in even asking if he could repaint his room. He was lying on his bed, flipping through next week's assignment in the algebra textbook, when he heard his father knock on the door.

"What is it, Dad?" he called back.

His dad opened the door and leaned in the doorway. "I wish you would call me *hairik*."

"And I wish you would call me Your Excellency." Alek had stopped using the Armenian words for *father* and *mother* years ago, and he had no intention of going back.

"Your brother and mother have left, and I'm going to make some sarma. You wanna watch?"

"Why don't you teach me how to make it myself?"

"Soon, Alek. Soon, but not yet."

Like every Khederian since the beginning of time, Nik had

waited until he was sixteen to be entrusted with the ancient Armenian art of rolling grapevine leaves. So even though it was Alek's favorite dish, until he turned sixteen and his parents decided he was ready, he'd have to settle for watching his father prepare it.

"Sure," Alek responded.

His father turned, and Alek followed him out of his room and down the stairs into the kitchen.

"How'd the job interview go?" Alek asked carefully.

"Well, I thought it went well, but since I haven't heard by now . . ." his father trailed off.

Since his dad had gotten fired from the architectural firm last year, Alek had probably spent more time with him than he had during the rest of his life. It's not that his father was entirely absent from those earlier memories. Just that his presence had been peripheral, more like a half-cropped figure in the background of a photograph.

Alek followed his father into the kitchen, the pride of every Armenian household. The shiny stainless steel refrigerator and matching dishwasher had been installed just weeks before Alek's father had been fired, and Alek knew that as soon as they could afford it, his mother was planning on upgrading the cabinets to cherrywood and the counter to granite.

Alek's father began assembling the sarma ingredients while Alek sat at the kitchen table.

"Alek, do you want to talk to me about anything?"

Alek's stomach sank, like he'd been lured into a trap that had just sprung open around him. "What do you mean?"

"I just want you to feel like you can tell me anything."

"I do."

"And if there's anything wrong, like with girls or even drugs or sex—"

"Oh my God, Dad, there's nothing wrong, okay?" Alek felt his face turn beet red. "I thought you were going to show me how you make sarma, not have a heart-to-heart, because even my algebra homework would be more enjoyable than that."

"Fine, fine, fine," his father said, equally relieved to change the subject. He joined Alek at the table and began making the Armenian delicacy. "Let me show you how to take these out without ripping them." He carefully finessed a wad of leaves from the glass jar, unfolded it, then removed one leaf at a time. Each one was dark and thin, with veins running down its length, like a human hand. "You want to make sure you use the California leaves, because they're sturdier than the Greek ones. Even still, the trick is to handle them very carefully. Like if you say the wrong thing, they might go running back to their room," his father joked.

Alek smiled in spite of himself. Other fathers might throw a softball around with their sons, or take them to hit at the tennis courts. But his quality time with his father involved being gently mocked while learning how to make Armenian dishes.

"Now, I use the scissors to cut off the little stub of stem at the bottom."

Alek's dad showed him how to make the stuffing for the leaves, a mixture of rice, lamb, spices, tomatoes, red peppers, chopped parsley, and olive oil. Then he spooned the stuffing onto the flat leaf and demonstrated how to fold and roll the leaf, creating a perfect little bundle of yumminess.

"Now I lay it gently in the pot."

"How come you always use the same pot whenever you make sarma?"

"This was the pot my mother always used to make sarma, and when I got married, she gave it to us. See how wide it is? Because of how the sarma cooks, you need a pot that's wide, not deep."

After a few minutes of working in silence, Alek's dad tried a new tactic. "I know your mother hasn't been around a lot lately, but try to be understanding with her."

"I am, Dad. She's the one who . . . As far as I'm concerned, she's the one who's messing everything up."

"Now, Alek, the way you're talking now—is that the kind of man you want to be?"

Alek knew there was only one right answer to this question. "No, Dad."

"Just remember—this is the first time she's worked full-time since before Nik was born. And most of the people at the UN have left since she was there, so she's working with new colleagues, and she's worried that no one is going to take her seriously. So whenever someone at the office has to stay late or pick up weekend hours, she volunteers so that they can see she's committed."

Alek didn't say anything. He just continued watching his father unwrap, snip, stuff, and roll.

"But more than her work, family is the most important thing for her. Like it is for me. And now it's time for us to support her the way she's supported us, okay?"

Alek didn't know why his dad's talking to him this way made him want to die. "Okay, Dad," he mumbled.

"And maybe we can all go to the city sometime soon. There's a Rodin exhibit at the Met. Does that sound good to you?"

Alek mumbled again, "Yes, Dad."

His father continued rolling in grateful silence. Finally, when all of the grapevine leaves were stuffed, rolled, and packed into the big pot, they filled it up halfway with hot water and brought it to a boil.

"Now we let it cook until it's done. Sometimes we add some tomato paste for extra flavor halfway through."

"That's how I like it."

"I know. So fifteen minutes before it's done cooking, you can add it today." Alek nodded his head, gratefully acknowledging even this small step in the journey of learning how to make sarma by himself.

"Dad, how long do you let it cook?"

"Just enough time."

"And how much tomato paste should I put in?"

"Not too much."

Alek rolled his eyes. He wondered if there were any Armenian cookbooks in the world, or if all of the recipes had to be learned this way.

6

FOUR DAYS LATER, ALEK PEELED HIS GAZE AWAY FROM the chalkboard and back into his algebra textbook. His lips were inexplicably dry, and he wished he had some lip balm so he wouldn't have to lick them every few seconds like a thirsty baby.

Mr. Weedin decided to end class by having a few Algebra II students work out a series of problems at the chalkboard. The Algebra I students were supposed to be working on their homework, but all Alek could do was try not to stare at Ethan.

The other students had finished solving their problems, but Ethan was still struggling with his. Alek copied Ethan's equation into his notebook and began working it through. But each time he tried, something didn't add up. After a few unsuccessful attempts, Alek raised his hand.

"Mr. Khederian, is this a question regarding your Algebra I

assignment?" Mr. Weedin asked him. "As you know, this is the Algebra II segment of the class, and I'd like to focus my attention on those students."

"Actually, Mr. Weedin, I couldn't help noticing the problem that Eth—all the way on the left side of the board. As it's written, it's impossible to solve."

"Is that so, Alek?"

"Yes, Mr. Weedin. But if you switch the second variable from a negative to a positive, which is what I think it's supposed to be, then the problem makes sense."

The Algebra I students looked up from their homework, and the upperclassmen in Algebra II redirected their attention from the chalkboard to Alek. This was the first time that Alek had spoken in class. Also, Mr. Weedin had a reputation for being meticulous, denying every extension request, and never making mistakes. Challenging him was momentous.

Mr. Weedin looked at Alek for a moment, then at the problem on the chalkboard, and then at his notes. The silence slowed time. As if in a trance, the class sat while Mr. Weedin checked his notes, making an arrhythmic clucking sound.

A few interminable moments later, Mr. Weedin cleared his throat. "You seem to be correct, Mr. Khederian."

The class gave a collective exhale.

"Don't worry, teach, I'm sure you'll get it right next time." Ethan smiled.

Mr. Weedin sheepishly walked to the board, made the necessary change, and Ethan solved the problem with a flourish.

Alek intentionally averted his eyes while Ethan walked back to his seat. Alek thought he saw Ethan lean toward him after sitting down as if he were going to say something, but the bell rang and Alek grabbed his bag and ran out of the classroom.

After his algebra triumph, Alek walked home with a swagger he hadn't felt that entire year. He wanted to share his victory with someone. But he couldn't tell his parents because they would've accused him of disrespecting his teacher. And he certainly wasn't going to tell Nik, who'd just find a way to use the story to belittle him.

Alek saw Orchard Street in the distance. He hadn't spoken to Becky since that awkward night last Friday when he tried to ask her advice about Ethan. He reached the intersection and paused, deliberating what to do. Sometimes, he decided, the easiest way to get over something was just to move forward. He made the turn and walked down the two blocks to Becky's house.

After ringing the doorbell twice, Alek heard Becky's footsteps scampering inside the house. A moment later, she opened the door.

"Um, Alek? You, uh, didn't call—I didn't know that you were, well, that you were coming." She avoided eye contact with Alek, nervously shifting her weight from one bare foot to the other. "Did we have plans?"

"Since when do I call before I come over?" Alek asked. "I want to tell you something."

"What is it?" Becky stood in the doorway, examining the doorknob as if it were an ancient artifact.

"Are you going to invite me in?"

"What're you, a vampire?" Becky shot back.

Alek took her joke as a good sign. He walked in and dropped his book bag. Becky's parents had met working at the same pharmaceutical laboratory outside of Princeton. Now their work took them all over the world, and they decorated their home with objects they collected from the international conventions they attended. A handwoven tablecloth from Ivory Coast depicting animals grazing at an oasis hung on the wall, over a modern Dutch sofa with no back. A Russian samovar, which Becky explained was an old-fashioned teapot, sat inside a Japanese tansu, next to a classic silver cup-and-saucer set that her parents had told Alek was from the Arts and Crafts period.

Alek started running down the steps to the basement.

"I'll meet you downstairs in a sec, okay?" Becky called out. Alek grabbed and popped open two Diet Dr Peppers from the little basement refrigerator. Becky loved Diet Dr Pepper so much, Alek sometimes saw her drinking it on the way to school in the morning. Her parents had tried to limit her intake, so Becky had taken to hiding cans in her room to make sure she could get her fix when she needed to. To Alek, Diet Dr Pepper tasted like Becky's basement.

Alek took his usual position on the sofa: on the right, with his feet up on the table. A few minutes later, Becky came down and sat next to him in her usual position: feet crossed on the sofa, snuggled into the corner between the back cushion and the armrest. Alek noticed she'd swept her hair back and taken her socks off.

"So, tell me what's going on," Becky said cautiously, as if Alek were the one who'd acted crazy the last time they hung out.

Alek recounted the entire Algebra class story, from the moment he noticed the mistake on the chalkboard to the way the bell rang the moment the incident was over. He took his time in the telling, hoping that by pretending that things were normal

60

between them, things would become normal between them. He even impersonated Mr. Weedin's British accent, knowing that Becky would get a kick out of it.

"He sounds just like Henry Higgins from *My Fair Lady!*" Becky said.

"That's exactly what I thought!"

"And this just happened today?" Becky asked.

"Yeah. I was walking home, and I passed your street, and I thought that there was no one in the world that I wanted to tell this to more than you."

Becky's eyes widened. "Really?"

"Of course, Becky. I don't think something counts until I've told you. These last few days made me realize how much I miss you, and how much you mean to me."

And she leaned over and kissed him.

Not a friendly, peck-on-the-cheek-because-we-got-into-a-fight-and-now-we're-making-up kiss. A full mouth-on-mouth kiss. The kiss lasted for a few seconds before Becky disengaged. Her face was still alarmingly close to Alek's, and he had to go cross-eyed to see her. Her eyes were wide. Alek had never seen them so wild.

Alek didn't know what to do, so he just sat there. He didn't mean to be encouraging, but that's how Becky must've taken it, because she leaned in again. Before her mouth could land on his, Alek put up his hands. He knew he couldn't kiss her again. "Don't."

Becky pulled back immediately, as if he'd shoved her. The excitement drained from her eyes, and her body went rigid. "I thought you wanted . . ."

Alek tried to choose his words carefully. "I don't know. If this. Is a good idea."

Becky's expression hardened. "Look, Alek, I think you really have to figure out what's going on here. Last week, you asked me if I've ever done something that scared the shit out of me. Then you blow me off for a week, and now you show up and tell me how much I mean to you, and how important I am . . ." Becky's eyes welled with tears. "Why are you messing with me like this?" she asked him.

"I'm not! I swear!" Alek couldn't understand what was going on. "I thought we were going to make up, not make out!" He could taste Becky's peppermint lip gloss on his lips. He couldn't believe that a few seconds ago her mouth had been on his. "You *are* my best friend, and you *are* that important to me—"

"I think you should go," Becky said, looking away from him. He could see she was exerting all of her willpower to keep the tears from spilling out of her eyes.

"But—"

"Alek. Go."

He had never heard such finality in her voice. Even last winter, when her grandfather died, she hadn't seemed this upset. Becky stood and ran up and out of the basement. He could hear her on the floor above him, then climbing the steps to the second floor of the house. Alek sat for a moment, unsure of what to do. He poured the rest of his Diet Dr Pepper down the basement sink, then tossed the can in the Boyces' recycling bin. He climbed up to the main floor of the house intending to continue up to Becky's room to bang on her door until she let him in. But then he saw she'd hung his book bag on the front doorknob. He got the message.

Alek made sure the door locked behind him.

The next day at lunch, Alek decided the cafeteria was the room he hated most in the world. The relentless fluorescent lighting gave everything a flat greenish hue, and even without the terrible school food being served, the place still smelled like wet socks. At least during the school year he had Becky to sit with and discuss the minutiae of their lives. But that kiss had changed everything.

Alek didn't know why it had unnerved him so much. He had kissed girls before. Maybe not recently, but that's because all of the freshman girls wanted to date upperclassmen boys, and the upperclassmen girls wouldn't even look at a freshman. In middle school, he'd had two girlfriends—Gail in seventh grade and Linsay in eighth. He had kissed Gail a few times and had made out with Linsay pretty seriously after Spring Fling. He still remembered the way she smelled that night, like flowers and sweat.

When his parents decided he couldn't try out for the tennis team, Alek promised to practice every day anyway. He hadn't kept his promise as religiously as he had wanted to, but more often than not, he'd made the time to hit against the wall in the basketball courts, run through his drills, or even get Jason or Matthew to volley with him. He missed tennis so much that he created the opportunity to have it in his life.

But that's not how he felt about kissing girls. It just wasn't something that he'd spent any time thinking about in high school. And when he asked himself why, he couldn't come up with a good reason. Probably, like everything else, it was another side effect of the misery that the last year had been. When high school stopped being a living hell, Alek figured, he'd get back to dating.

"What're you eating, dude? That shit smells funky."

Alek looked up and saw Ethan leaning on the other side of the cafeteria table, his blue eyes staring at him intensely. Alek's heart started racing.

"What?" He choked.

"I said, what're you eating? That's no hoagie."

Alek wanted to die. Finally, Ethan was talking to him, and the first thing they were going to discuss was the weird food his parents packed him.

"This is Armenian string cheese," Alek said, holding up a long braid of white cheese flecked with black spots.

"Like Polly-O?"

"Um, sorta. You unwrap it like this." Alek demonstrated by unpeeling a strip of the cheese down the length of its spiral braid. He was grateful to have something to do.

"What's that black shit?"

"The specks? They're spices. They give it a little kick."

"Lemme see." Ethan shone a miniature LED bulb attached to one of the chains looped around his low-hanging cargo shorts and used it to examine the cheese.

"You come prepared, don't you?" Alek observed.

"Jewelers use these lights to inspect diamonds. They're perfect for when you're clubbing, and it's dark and the music's blasting, but you need to see. You know?"

Alek nodded his head knowingly, although he'd never actually been clubbing.

"And more importantly," Ethan continued, "they're perfect for investigating unidentified speckled cheese. Can I try it?" he asked solemnly.

"Go for it," Alek answered with an equal amount of solemnity.

After a few attempts, Ethan got the hang of unraveling the cheese. "This tastes pretty awesome, man. Definitely better than the shitty slices of American my dad picks up at the supermarket."

Alek felt a wave of gratitude wash over him, for everyone from his father, who packed today's lunch, to the Armenian who first invented string cheese.

"Anyway, dude, I just wanted to thank you for doing me that solid."

"That what?"

"You know, a solid. It means . . ." Ethan searched for the definition. "Basically, it means you did me a favor, and I wanted to give you props for that. Like if I said, 'I wanna give my boy Alek a shout-out for doing me a solid in Mr. W's Alge class.' It means 'thank you.' *Capisce*?"

"Cap what?"

"*Capisce.* It's how mobsters say 'understand?' " Ethan looked at Alek with surprise. "Don't you watch TV?"

"My parents only let me watch half an hour a day."

"What!"

"Yeah. They think television is rotting the minds of the people in this country."

"So what do you do?"

"Well, I used to play tennis. And I go to the movies."

"Your parents don't think that movies are rotting the minds of the people in this country?"

"They probably do, but at least this way they get me out of the house."

Ethan laughed. Alek couldn't believe how quickly Ethan morphed from being an unapproachable D.O. to someone he could talk to.

"Anyway, dude, thanks. If I don't pass Alge they'll make me repeat, and that wouldn't fly well with Father, ya hear?"

"I hear," Alek responded, playing along.

"And thanks for the cheese, Polly-O."

"It's not Polly-O. My parents would never buy Polly-O."

"No, fool. That's gonna be my name for you from now on. 'Cause like string cheese, you're wound up tight."

Alek's heart sank at the description.

"But you also got flecks that give you flavor." Ethan winked.

And his heart soared again.

"Peace out, Polly-O."

Ethan made his way back to his cafeteria table. Alek could see the elastic band of Ethan's underwear peeking out of his shorts, almost as if the purple 2(X)IST label were winking at Alek and anyone else bold enough to witness it. Looking down at his own boring denim shorts, Alek could never imagine wearing pants that low, especially since Principal Saunder's dress code prohibited them. During the school year, it might even earn Ethan a suspension, but in the summer, everything was looser.

. . .

Walking to school five days later, Alek braced himself as he passed Becky's street. It's not like he thought she was going to be waiting for him or anything, but seeing Orchard Street reminded him of how he and Becky still hadn't talked, and he knew that the more time that passed, the harder it would be. He supposed he could've reached out to her, but since she'd been the one who kicked him out of her house, he thought it wouldn't kill her to make the first move.

Alek reached the train station and decided to risk being a few minutes late to English so he could witness the 8:17 on its way up to the city. He ran up the stairs to the platform.

"Check it, Polly-O!" he heard a familiar voice call out from the other side.

Ethan! Looking across, he saw him hanging off the railing on the opposite side of the station, his book bag casually slung over his shoulders.

"Hey, Ethan!" Alek called back. Seeing him made Alek smile.

Ethan looked around conspiratorially, and then beckoned to Alek to come to him. Alek ran up the overpass and found Ethan examining a New York City subway map.

"Have fun in Alge today. And don't mention the running-into-me thing, okay?"

"What do you mean?"

"Figure it out, Polly-O. I'm at a train station. When school starts in fifteen minutes, you're going to be sitting in some lame-ass classroom, and I'll be on my way to the Big Apple."

"You're cutting?" Alek asked incredulously.

"Hell yeah."

"So why are you going into the city?" Alek said, trying to

67

sound nonchalant. He might not be able to go there on his own, but he knew it would be way uncool to refer to it as "New York City." Everyone just called it "the city," as if to imply that the rest of the so-called cities, like Chicago or Los Angeles or Boston, didn't really count.

"There's this concert series in the park. Rufus Wainwright was supposed to play last Monday, but he got sick and had to bail. He felt so bad for his loyal fans like me, though, that he decided to do an impromptu thing today instead."

Alek wouldn't admit he didn't know who Rufus Wainwright was, so he just said, "Cool." He searched his memory quickly and came up with the first thing about New York that popped into his head. "You know, I hear there's a great Rodin exhibit at the Metropolitan Museum."

Ethan looked impressed. "Really?"

Encouraged, Alek went on. "Sure. I'm dying to check it out."

A mischievous glint entered Ethan's eyes. "Why don't you come with me?"

"What?"

"Come with me. The Met's right off Central Park. We can hit the concert, check out the exhibit, and be back before the bell rings."

"No way." Alek didn't even have to think about it. As alluring as the idea of spending that Tuesday with Ethan in New York was, he would never cut school.

"Why not?"

"For one thing, I don't have enough money."

"Bullshit. You got ten bucks?"

"Yeah."

"That's all you'll need."

"But what about the ticket for the concert, or the train ride, or—"

"Shut up. I said you could do it on ten bucks, so you can do it on ten bucks. Or don't you trust me?"

"I trust you."

"So what's the problem?"

Alek's mind raced, but the sound of the train approaching in the distance was making thinking difficult.

"Polly-O, don't be such a pussy." Ethan raised his voice over the sound of the approaching train. "Have some fun."

For a second, Alek actually found himself thinking about what it would be like to forget about school and his teachers and parents, even for just a day, and go on this adventure. But he just wasn't that kind of guy.

The train pulled into the station. Ethan waited for everyone else to board, then got on. "Any chance I can persuade you?" he asked Alek from across the portal.

"Sorry, man."

"No prob, dude. Maybe next time." Ethan held out his hand to snap Alek's fingers goodbye. But when their hands met, Ethan interlocked his fingers around Alek's wrist. Ethan pulled back with all of his strength, yanking Alek onto the train. Alek, stunned, didn't even try to break Ethan's hold as he heard the doors *beep-beep* close behind him. Alek turned around and saw South Windsor move away as the train started speeding to New York.

7

"THIS IS KIDNAPPING! I CAN'T BELIEVE IT!" ALEK exclaimed.

"It's for your own good."

"But I don't even have a ticket. And how'm I going to get back in time for school?"

"You really want to go back?" Ethan asked, leaning in, his eyes daring Alek.

"There's no 'want' here, Ethan. I *have* to get back," Alek insisted.

"Alek, my man, at a certain point in your life, you're gonna learn there's a difference between what you *have* to do and what you *want* to do. And the sooner you start choosing *want* over *have*, the happier you'll be." Ethan stretched, his arms unfolding above him like wings. "So if you really *want*, you can get off in five minutes at Princeton Junction, switch directions on the next outbound train, and be back at school five minutes late, max. But is that what you *want*?"

Alek gathered his thoughts as the train gained momentum, the landscape on either side accelerating to a blur. He took his Velcro wallet out of his pocket and displayed its inhabitants, a pair of wrinkled five-dollar bills. "You sure I can do this on ten dollars?"

His audacity earned him Ethan's most winning smile. "You will find that I am a man of my word. Keep up."

Wading through the commuters in their business casual attire, Alek followed Ethan to the bathroom on the other side of the car. Ethan leaned forward and whispered in Alek's ear. "Go in there, close the door behind you, and lock it. When you hear me knock four times, unlock it quickly and step back."

"What?"

"Don't ask questions now, just do what I tell you."

"But—"

"Shut up! Do you see him?" Ethan pointed to the train ticket collector, who was slowly making his way over to them, punching tickets as he went.

"Yeah."

"Lesson the first: if you want to spend a whole day in New York City on ten dollars, you don't pay for the train ticket."

"But isn't that stealing?"

"Lesson the second: if no one suffers, it's not bad."

Alek protested. "My parents are always saying there's no such thing as a victimless crime."

Ethan rolled his eyes. "If you spend your only coin getting to the city, you won't have any left to do anything fun once you actually get there. So just do what I tell you to, okay?"

Alek nodded his consent, and Ethan dropped down and took some Scotch tape, a thick black marker, and a piece of white construction paper out of his bag. With the marker, he quickly scrawled *OUT OF ORDER* on the paper.

"What are you waiting for? Go!" Ethan opened the bathroom door, shoved Alek in, and slammed it shut behind him.

Alek flicked the metal latch, locking himself into the bathroom. The compartment was small, but fortunately not dirty or smelly. He positioned himself awkwardly, crouching in the corner, the metal wall cold through his shirt. He waited, not knowing what to do.

A few moments stretched into an uncomfortable anxiety, and Alek started getting genuinely scared. What if Ethan was setting him up—pulling him on the train, then abandoning him in the bathroom? What if Ethan got off at the next stop, stranding Alek on the train by himself? Would Alek spend the rest of the trip locked in the bathroom? And how would he get back home after, let alone explain to his parents why he cut school and ended up on a train to New York?

Alek put his hand on the door and was about to let himself out when he heard the four distinct raps. He unlocked the door and stepped back quickly, barely avoiding the swinging door. Ethan snuck in and dropped the latch, locking the door behind him. He hopped on the little steel sink, letting his feet dangle.

"So what, we spend the entire ride in here?" Alek asked.

"You got it. That Out of Order sign means we won't be

bothered since nobody knows what the hell is going on in these trains. Consider this our private suite for the next forty-five minutes."

"Are you kidding me?" Alek could've never conceived of a scheme like this, let alone have the audacity to execute it.

"You don't have to sound so impressed—it's not like I came up with it myself. But it works like a charm. You just have to make sure that no one sees you put the sign up. The rest is cake. Of course, sometimes this place smells like shit, literally, and then you're in for one hell of a ride. But it's still free."

"Whoever showed you this must be a genius."

"Yeah, he was." Ethan's mouth tightened. He sat quietly and looked straight ahead, away from Alek.

Forty-five minutes later, the train pulled into Penn Station, and Alek and Ethan ducked out of the bathroom, camouflaging themselves among the throngs of passengers making their way out of the train. A fluorescent glare greeted them when they emerged from the underground stairwell.

"Welcome to Pennsylvania Station," Ethan said wryly. "Or, as I like to call it, Pee-Stain, because that's what it looks and smells like."

Alek laughed. It wasn't an inaccurate description.

"You should check out some pictures of what this place was originally, before they ripped it down in the sixties and put up this nasty piece of concrete shit," Ethan lamented. "I wish that instead of coming into Pee-Stain, NJ Trans went into G-C instead."

"G-C?"

"Grand Central. It's the train station on the east side of town. That's how cool New York is—it gets *two* train stations. G-C is exactly what you expect a New York train station to look like—columns, gilding, the whole beautiful turn-of-the-century thing. And, on the ceiling, they've re-created the night sky, star for star, constellation for constellation. We can check it out the next time we come into the city."

Let's just survive this trip first, Alek thought, *before we commit to another.* But he didn't want Ethan to realize how scared he was, so instead he said, "You come into the city a lot?" He worked hard to pitch his voice to sound casual.

"Used to all the time." Ethan increased the speed at which he was walking, weaving his way through the crowd like he was on his skateboard. Alek had to practically run to keep up. "I took a break for a while, but now I'm thinking of resuming the habit."

A few minutes later, Alek followed Ethan down some stairs and ramps to the subway entrance. Ethan walked up to the MetroCard machine, which Alek thought was only a joystick away from looking exactly like an old-school arcade video game, its patches of primary colors accentuated by the sleek metal exterior.

"Wouldn't it be easier to just stand in line at the booth?" Alek asked.

"That's *so* tourist," Ethan responded. "Now give me one of your fivers."

Alek slipped one of his two precious bills to Ethan, who matched it with a five-dollar bill of his own and fed both into the machine. Then he expertly navigated his way through the touch screen until a yellow card popped out.

"Don't I get one?" Alek asked.

Ethan looked him up and down. "Where does all of your paranoia come from, man?"

Alek looked away, embarrassed. "I just thought—"

"Trust me, okay? I brought you in here, and I'm gonna take care of you. *Capisce?*"

"Capisce," Alek responded.

"Now I'm gonna swipe, and you walk through. Got it?" Alek nodded. "Wait for my go."

When a crowd of commuters walked by, Ethan nodded to Alek, lining up at the turnstile. Alek waited for Ethan's swipe, then began walking through the portal. Before the bar rotated forward, he felt Ethan sneak in behind, the front of his body pressing against the back of Alek's.

"Don't stop," Ethan hissed, and the two of them emerged on the other side of the threshold, the bar rotating behind them. "That's my two-for-one subway special. One of the many money-saving tips you'll learn from me today, young grasshopper."

Alek nodded appreciatively, still feeling the sensation of Ethan's body against his.

"I've never taken the subway before," Alek admitted while they were waiting on the platform. "My folks sometimes drive us in, but then we park in a lot, and if we need to get around we cab it."

"Lesson the third: never take a cab."

"Why not?"

"Hella pricey, first of all. But more importantly, real New Yorkers take the subway. Or Citibike. Look at the people standing here waiting with us."

Alek looked up and down the waiting platform, absorbing the colorful scene. An old Chinese man was playing an instrument that looked like a cello's skeleton with just one big string and sounded like a sad ghost trying to communicate with the living. Three African-American girls around Alek's age were animatedly discussing the boys in their school.

"Girl, if you even think about touchin' Ramen, I'm gonna yank that cheap weave out."

"I know Ramen's yours. And besides, I wouldn't touch him with any of these fingers." The second girl flashed her purple, manicured nails for emphasis. "He's a dog."

The first girl's protests didn't disturb a young Arab man sitting on a bench reading a textbook on the history of board games. Lots of men and women in clothes similar to what Alek's mother wore to work, like the people on the train from South Windsor, were waiting in between old couples and young couples and middle-aged couples with babies. Alek felt the self-consciousness that always hung over him evaporate. Who would possibly pay attention to him when there was so much else to take in?

"You see shit here you'd never see anywhere else," Ethan said proudly, as if he'd arranged for the display.

The sound of the approaching subway thundered throughout the station. Alek and Ethan boarded. The carriage was so crowded that they had to stand right next to each other. When the train stalled abruptly, Alek lost his balance and almost fell on top of Ethan.

"I'm sorry, I'm so sorry," Alek started blubbering.

"You don't have to apologize. I don't mind," Ethan said. Alek felt his face go red and looked away immediately. He tried to find some space to maneuver into, but the subway car was packed full. Alek could feel Ethan's clothes rub up against his body.

"Do you know where we're going?" Alek asked nervously.

"Course I do."

"Will you show me on your map?"

"Absolutely not."

"Why not?"

"Lesson the fourth: never look at a subway map in front of other people. It's like getting up and screaming, 'Take advantage of me! I don't live in New York!'" Ethan whispered.

"But we *don't* live in New York!" Alek whispered back.

"No one has to know that. You know what the biggest compliment in the world is? When someone asks you for directions. It means that you really look like you know where you're going." Ethan leaned in. "We stay on the C train for four stops, then we get off and we walk through Central Park to SummerStage. Until then, kick back, relax, and look cool." Alek did his best to follow Ethan's instructions.

When they climbed out of the subway stop a few minutes later, Alek found himself in front of the entrance to Central Park.

"You see that building?" Ethan asked, pointing to a palatial structure across the street. "That's the Dakota. It's, like, the fanciest building in New York."

"Dakota like Dakota Fanning?"

"No, fool. Dakota like the states, because when it was built, like, a hundred years ago, going this far uptown was considered undiscovered country, like going to North Dakota," Ethan said. "At least, that's what people say."

"How do you know so much about the city?"

"You hang out enough, you pick things up." Ethan waited for a gap in traffic, and before the red Don't Walk turned to the white Walk, he bounded across the avenue. Alek considered saying that his parents had always taught him to wait for the Walk, but decided against it and followed Ethan, close in tow, into the impossible forest universe that was Central Park.

"We're a little early, so we're gonna take the scenic route," Ethan informed him.

Walking through the park, Alek and Ethan passed people feeding goats and sheep at a petting zoo, paddling little boats over the lakes, jogging along the park's circumference, reading plaques under statues of literary figures, and picnicking on the grass.

"The park rocks because it's the best of both worlds: city and country at the same time."

Alek nodded his consent. He couldn't believe that just a few minutes ago he'd been underground, wading through a sea of commuters on a subway. All he could make out of urban Manhattan now was the tops of skyscrapers peeking above the trees. In this section of the park, there weren't even any roads for cars— just walkways for bikers and runners and skaters.

"I can't wait to tell Becky about all the Rollerbladers in Central Park!" Alek said, adding a silent *if I ever speak to her again.*

"Becky who?"

"Becky Boyce—we always sit together at lunch."

"No idea who you're talking about, man," Ethan said, admiring a large collection of boulders, each the size of a small house, that looked like they'd been there since the prehistoric age.

Alek stopped walking. "Ethan, when did you become aware I existed?"

"That day that Jack almost kicked your ass."

"Never before then?"

"We go to school with twelve hundred other kids. It's not like you know who everybody is either," Ethan said. "How about you? What's your first memory of me?"

Alek had known Ethan existed from his first days of school. It was hard to miss him, walking through the school like he owned it.

"Well, you know, you have a certain notoriety . . ."

"I do?" Ethan asked with the perfect balance of humility and pride.

"Well, you were responsible for the single most chaotic event in recent school history."

Ethan laughed again. "One little food fight and suddenly that's all people know."

By the time they arrived at the outdoor stage, a large crowd had already gathered. Alek could feel the anticipation in the air before the first fork of lightning erupted from a storm cloud. He unsuccessfully tried to locate the ticket booth.

"You know I've only got five bucks left," Alek told Ethan.

"You gotta chill out, dude."

"So what, we're going to sneak into the concert without tickets? And you're going to convince me that's okay, too?"

"Who needs to sneak? It's free."

"What?"

"All of these awesome things are totally free in the summer— swing dancing at Lincoln Center, movies in Bryant Park, yoga along Riverside Park. Lots of people leave New York in the summer 'cause it's so humid and nasty, but it's my favorite time to be in the city."

Alek assumed that the audience would consist of young people, like himself and Ethan, but he was surprised to discover that the audience was as diverse as the subway crowd. He wondered how all these grownups were free to attend a concert in the middle of a Tuesday. Didn't they have jobs? Standing right next to him was a middle-aged couple holding a grocery bag. They were old enough to be his parents, waiting for the show to start with as much excitement as anyone else. The only major difference Alek could make out between the subway and the concert crowds was that here in the park, he could see men holding hands with each other.

Alek tried to remember if he'd ever seen two guys holding hands before. Girls did it all the time at school, of course, but not boys. And he'd certainly seen gay characters on TV and in movies. But as live viewings went, he concluded this was his first time. And like everything else in New York City, there was so much else going on that the sight of men holding hands didn't even warrant a second look from anyone else.

The crowd erupted into applause the moment they saw Rufus. He didn't wait for the noise to die down. He jumped right into his first song, crooning the words *"Who are you, New York?"* to his adoring fans.

"Have you ever seen Rufus perform before?" Ethan asked Alek. Alek shook his head no, too embarrassed to admit that this was the first bona fide concert that he had ever attended. "He's this amazing indie singer/songwriter/composer. He even wrote an opera!" Ethan gushed.

Rufus was wearing a striped white-and-purple shirt, open to the third button, with a white cravat tucked inside. A flower was pinned to the lapel of his linen jacket, and tight pants hugged his legs as he strutted onstage, strumming his guitar and caressing the words with his voice. Even though Alek knew he was just one of the hundreds, maybe thousands of people in the audience, he felt like Rufus was singing just to him.

Alek couldn't tell if it was the radiant sun, or all of the cool people, or getting to hang out with Ethan, but at some point he gave up trying to figure out why he was having such a great time and just surrendered to the perfect afternoon.

Ethan was clearly a die-hard Rufus fan: he knew every word to every song and danced along to most of them. Sometimes, Ethan would just bop along by himself. For the fast songs, he'd join groups of people dancing, drifting his way into the crowd. But he'd never be gone so long that Alek felt self-conscious about being alone. Ethan only remained still during Rufus's final encore, "Do I Disappoint You." By the crowd's reaction, Alek could tell this was one of his signature songs. Even people who couldn't sing along to anything else knew the words to this one, and Alek joined in for the last refrain, singing *"Do I disappoint you?"* along with everyone else.

The words clearly had a deeper meaning to Ethan, who looked off into the distance while the song played. Occasionally, Ethan's lips would mouth along some of the lyrics, but he never actually made any sound. Alek wanted to ask about the song's significance, but Ethan looked so solemn that Alek decided against it.

Two encores later, Rufus was forced to say, "I love you all, I do, but if I don't leave now you'll never let me." He took one final bow to thunderous applause and ran off the stage. Even still, Alek heard people screaming, "I love you, Rufus!" and "Come back!" He even heard someone in the audience ask Rufus to marry him, but nothing was going to make everyone's favorite rock star come back on the stage.

When the concert ended, the audience started dispersing, packing up their picnics and blankets and portable plastic lawn chairs. Two guys making out remained seated on the ground, oblivious to their surroundings. If Alek had never seen two men holding hands before, he'd certainly never seen them kiss.

"Rufus is a homo, so his music is really popular with faggots," Ethan whispered to Alek conspiratorially.

Alek couldn't believe what he heard. He looked at Ethan, waiting for him to apologize or make a joke, but he didn't say anything. Alek realized that even though he felt like he'd known Ethan for years, he probably didn't know him at all. The person he thought he knew would never use that kind of hateful language.

"You ready to go to the museum?" Ethan continued nonchalantly.

Alek nodded yes.

"Everything okay, dude?"

"Sure," Alek grunted.

Alek and Ethan walked through the park, passed a statue of Samuel Morse, and exited on the opposite side.

"We'll walk up Fifth Avenue to get to the museum," Ethan informed Alek. "It's only ten blocks away. You know how long that'll take us?"

Alek shook his head.

"Ten minutes exactly—each street takes around one minute to walk, and each avenue around four. Sometimes it gets trickier to figure out, like on the East Side where the Avenues get shorter, but that's the basic rule for figuring out pedestrian commute time in the city."

Alek could tell that Ethan was proud of his equation. And even though Alek was impressed by it, he wasn't going to give Ethan the satisfaction of saying so.

They walked up Fifth Avenue, with Central Park on their left and tall residential buildings stretching into the sky on their right.

"The Met starts what's known as Musuem Mile." Ethan walked briskly with his hands in his pockets. "It starts at 82nd Street and goes all the way up to 105th. You want me to show you on the map?"

If it had been earlier in the day, before Ethan had used the F-word, Alek would've said yes immediately. "I thought we weren't supposed to look at maps in Manhattan," Alek shot back instead.

"Nobody's looking at us, so it wouldn't violate lesson the fourth."

When Alek caught sight of the majestic building, he walked ahead of Ethan, past the used-book and hot-dog vendors, up the stairs so wide they could've been the footprint to a separate building altogether. Having been to the Metropolitan Museum of Art before and having a sense of where it was, Alek was relieved he didn't need Ethan to guide him.

"Wait up, man," Ethan called after him.

"I just want to get this over with as soon as possible."

"What's the rush?" Ethan asked, taken aback.

Alek continued charging forward, not bothering to answer.

When he entered the museum lobby he got in line, Ethan right behind him.

"That'll be twenty-four dollars for the both of you," the young man inside the glass booth said.

Alek looked up and saw the large sign clearly displaying the admission cost: $25 for adults, $17 for seniors, and $12 for students. He should've known Ethan's claim that this trip could be done in ten dollars was a lie.

"But you gotta let us in as long as we give you something, right?" Ethan asked knowingly.

"Excuse me?"

"I mean, if we decide just to pay this," Ethan said as he slid two dimes over the counter, "you still have to admit us, right?"

The counter person's tone quickly changed from polite to annoyed as he puffed up. "I mean, I guess so," he sputtered. "But the suggested donation for two students really is twenty-four dollars."

"Luckily, I don't really need other people's suggestions. I've got enough of my own. You wanna give us those pins?"

"Actually, we use stickers now."

"Well, cough up two stickers then." Ethan appeared oblivious to the line he was holding up behind him.

The counter person begrudgingly slid two little yellow stickers with the Metropolitan *M* boldly emblazed in the middle. Alek imitated Ethan by slapping it on his shirt pocket.

They walked past the guard, who saw their stickers and nodded for them to enter. In spite of how offended Alek still was by the word, he couldn't help complimenting Ethan.

"I can't believe you pulled that off."

"Me either," Ethan admitted. "I'd heard that you could get away with it, but I never actually had the balls to give it a go. I didn't think that punk-ass ticket guy was gonna let us. Did you see the look on his face?"

"Totally. So why'd he let us in?"

"The admission here is just a suggested donation, which is different from a ticket price. A suggested donation is 'we really hope you pay this much, but if you don't we can't actually stop you from coming in.'"

"You know everything!" Alek cried.

"My dad teaches sociology at NYU. My mom split when I was six, and ever since then he'd bring me in whenever he had night classes because he didn't want to pay for a sitter. Then I started coming in by myself when I was eleven. I used to sit in the back of his class bored as hell, so when I got old enough he let me out to explore. I know this city better than most people who grew up here. It's my playground."

Alek followed Ethan into the Rodin exhibit. The black bronze statues were laid out in a large open room, making it feel like they were in a garden. The first one they saw was an enormous framed doorway portal, made of writhing figures that looked like they were trying to explode out of the structure. "This one is called *The Gates of Hell*," Ethan said, reading the placard next to it. "That's what I feel like every time I walk into school," he joked. Alek was about to agree, but then he remembered that he was mad at Ethan. He mumbled noncommittally and walked away instead.

Alek let himself get lost in the bronze figures. He found that the sculptures changed depending on the angle from which he was looking at them. Other times, the essence of the piece was the same even when the perspective was not, like *The Shade*, whose tortured neck and head succeeded in evoking anguish in Alek regardless of where he stood. To appreciate other sculptures, like *The Athlete*, Alek had to get in close so he could see the detail in the figure's perfectly proportioned body.

Alek finished making his way through the exhibit over an hour and a half after he started. He was worried that Ethan was going to want to stay longer, so he was relieved when he heard him say, "I used to think that I hated going to museums because I'd spend the whole day inside and be so sick of it by the end that I wanted to puke. But now I just go, catch one exhibit, then get out. It's better that way."

"Sounds good to me," Alek agreed. "I've had enough."

Alek and Ethan sat rigidly in the bathroom of the NJ Transit train heading back to South Windsor. The regular *chut-chut-chut* of the train against the track and a leaky faucet were the only sounds they could hear. A drop of water lazily accumulated at the mouth of the nozzle, then eventually plopped itself down into the sink.

Alek focused on the forming droplet, counting in his head how many seconds it took to accumulate enough weight to fall.

"You got any plans this week?" Ethan asked.

"Nope," Alek responded.

"I'm thinking about heading into the city again."

A few minutes passed before Ethan spoke again. "You gonna tell your parents about today?"

"No," Alek said, without shifting his eyes from the sink.

"My dad doesn't really care," Ethan bragged.

Another awkward silence followed, until Ethan asked, "You want me to show you how to forge a note from your folks to the guidance counselor?"

"No, thanks."

After fifteen drops (approximately forty to fifty-two seconds per drop, assuming the train didn't lurch and jostle it prematurely), Ethan turned to Alek.

"Okay, Polly-O, I just gotta ask—why're you being such a dick?"

"You're the dick, Ethan," Alek fired back.

"What're you talking about?"

"I'm not the one who goes around using words like *faggot*."

Ethan looked stunned for a second, then burst out laughing. Alek stood up and put his hand on the bathroom handle. He was so infuriated that he didn't think he could be in the same space as Ethan.

"Alek, I'm going to explain something to you. Please stop me if you know what I'm going to say, okay?" Alek gave the barest of nods, and Ethan continued. "When you're, like, a member of a certain . . ." Ethan trailed off, trying to find the words. "Let me put it this way. Take the N-word."

Alek looked at him, appalled. "That's another word that I don't think it would be okay for you to use. Are you trying to offend me?"

"I'm just using it as an example," Ethan responded quickly. "But if you heard me drop the N-bomb, that wouldn't be right."

"No, it wouldn't."

"But you've heard one black guy use that word when talking to another black guy, right?"

"Sure, but that's different."

"How come?"

Alek searched to articulate something he intuitively knew to be true. "When you're part of a group, you can use words that would be inappropriate otherwise," Alek finally managed.

"Exactly!" Ethan exclaimed triumphantly. "I couldn't have put it better myself. That's why it's okay for me to use the word *faggot*."

"But that would only be okay if you were actually . . ."

"Gay. I'm gay," Ethan said, surprised. "I thought you . . ."

"What?" Alek asked.

"I thought you knew. No biggie, man."

Alek leaned back and cataloged his Ethan interactions. When he thought about the comments Ethan made, like not minding when their bodies collided into each other on the subway, or how comfortable Ethan was dancing with other men at the Rufus concert, it all made sense.

"You coo' with that?" Ethan asked.

"Yeah, of course. I mean, sure I'm cool with it. It's not like I'm homophobic or anything," Alek stumbled. It wasn't a big deal. He just hadn't had any gay friends, but then again, who did at fourteen? This was probably around the age people would start coming out, Alek figured.

"I gotta tell you, Polly-O, I love that you were going to break up with me because I said *faggot*."

"Break up with you?"

"Of course. A friend breakup. Those happen just like other

ones. And you were going to do it because I used the word *faggot*. That takes balls, man. Big balls."

Alek blushed. "I have to do what I think is right."

"Like cutting school today? Was that the right thing to do?"

"Not like that. I mean, when I have two options, and one of them is obviously the capital-R *Right* thing—the honest thing, the thing your gut tells you is right?"

Ethan nodded yes.

"Well, in those situations, I have to do that thing. It's like something inside of me stops me from doing anything else. Trust me. I've tried. It's not possible. I have to do the Right thing."

"I get it, man. You're gonna stick by your principles." Ethan grinned at Alek. "I admire a man with principles. But still, I gotta ask you. Was cutting today the Right thing to do?"

Alek thought for a moment.

"Yeah." He smiled. "I think it was."

8

"DO YOU MIND SIGNING THIS?" ALEK ASKED HIS FATHER before anyone else came home, sliding over the math test he'd salvaged from the wastepaper basket under his desk. His father unglued his eyes from the computer screen where he'd been reformatting his résumé.

"Why do I need to sign a ninety-three?" he asked.

"To prove I showed it to you. Mr. Weedin is a total nazi about these things," Alek said.

"That's not funny, Alek. You shouldn't go throwing around words like that so casually." His dad absentmindedly signed the test. "Now, you think you can help me with this?" His dad gestured to the computer screen. "I can't get the fields to line up."

"You're such a dinosaur," Alek said, grabbing the keyboard and aligning the tabs. "I don't know how old people like you get anything done."

Alek's father chuckled. "You know, I felt that way when I was your age and I had to help my parents with typewriters. And your children will feel that way, too, when the technology has evolved faster than you can keep up with it."

After saving his dad's document, Alek ran up to his room, making sure the yellow MetroCard Ethan had given him and the Metropolitan Museum Sticker were discreetly hidden in the drawer where he kept all of his sentimentally valuable objects, like the tennis ball from the final match with Seth and the silver Armenian cross he'd received from his grandmother when he was baptized.

He took out the printed excuse note he'd already typed up and placed it over his dad's signature on the math test, just as Ethan had told him. When he held the documents up to the lamp, he could trace the signature from the test perfectly on the forged note. Then he stood in front of his bedroom mirror, practicing exactly what he'd say to Principal Saunder's secretary the next day when he handed her the note. "I woke up with a fever yesterday and my dad thought it would be better if I stayed home. It broke last night, and he said I could take another day off just to make sure I was feeling okay, but I didn't want to miss any more school." He spent the entire night preparing his speech.

He even got to school fifteen minutes early, but all of his precautions proved unnecessary when Principal Saunder's secretary accepted the note without even asking for an explanation. She made the appropriate mark in her computer, and, just like that, Alek had been excused for his cut day. He floated through English in the morning, barely able to concentrate on the lesson. Everything in South Windsor felt insignificant and two-dimensional now, like an outdated video game version of itself.

When Alek walked into the cafeteria for lunch, he went to his usual seat by himself. For a second, he thought about what it would be like if Ethan invited him to sit at the D.O. table, but he knew that would never happen. One by one, they strutted into the cafeteria, performing even mundane activities aggressively. Alek couldn't imagine how to make the act of buying a soda from the machine menacing.

Finally, Ethan walked in. But his swagger didn't have its usual bounce. His eyes were bloodshot, his floppy hair disheveled, and his clothes were so rumpled, it looked like he'd slept in them. The other Dropouts didn't appear to notice or comment on Ethan's mood. A guy with spiky bleached-blond hair delivered the punch line to a joke, and the guys erupted with laughter, pounding their fists on the table.

Alek continued watching Ethan for the entirety of lunch. A few minutes before the period ended, Ethan walked over to the ice cream machine, and Alek jumped at the opportunity to approach him alone.

"Hey, Ethan!"

"Wassup, Alek."

"Not much."

Ethan was staring at the ice cream machine. His body was turned away from Alek, slumped against the machine, as if deciding between an ice cream sandwich and a Popsicle were as important as choosing which college to attend.

"Well, I just wanted to tell you that I had a great time yesterday, and I really wanted to thank you for . . ."

Alek stopped speaking when he saw Ethan turn and look past

him. Jack and another D.O., with a red knit cap pulled down to his eyes, stood behind Alek, looking like ravenous hyenas that had just spotted a fresh carcass, ripe for devouring. Alek prayed that they hadn't overheard what he had said.

"I had a great time, too, Ethan," the one with the red knit cap said to Ethan coyly, then started faux-kissing Jack, the meaty D.O. who'd shoved Alek in the parking lot. Jack cracked up in response. "Thanks for last night," he managed through cackles. Ethan started laughing along with them. Alek could feel his face turn bright red, and he froze with embarrassment.

The two guys walked past Alek, giving him a shove on the way, like he wasn't even there. "Eth, we'll see you on the ramps after school."

"Don't think I'm gonna make it, Pedro. Catch you tomorrow."

"No prob, dude. Later," Pedro called back, throwing Ethan a peace sign goodbye. "And I really did have a great time yesterday," he snickered. Pedro and Jack started cracking up again as they bounded out of the cafeteria. Ethan turned back to Alek.

"Alek, why don't we chill later? Maybe—"

"Maybe what? We can hang out again when you're not around your real friends?"

"What the hell are you talking about, dude?"

"Go to hell, Ethan."

Alek ran back to his table, grabbed his despised green book bag, and bolted out of the cafeteria. He knew that he was supposed to go to Algebra class, but there was no way he would be in the same room as Ethan, let alone sit next to him, after what had just happened.

. . .

An hour later, cars whizzed by Alek on the highway shoulder as he faced the large red Dairy Queen sign. He hadn't known this was where his feet would take him.

He snuck his way to the side of the building, hiding behind a large human-sized banana split cutout. He spied Becky serving a stick-thin middle-aged woman whose gray roots showed through her patchily dyed orange hair.

"Do you know how many carbs the Blizzard has?" the woman asked in a piercing, nasal voice.

"Ninety-two grams per serving," Becky answered dutifully.

"And how many ounces in a serving?"

"Ten and a half."

"And do you base that information on the Oreo Cookies Blizzard or the Chocolate Chip Cookie Dough Blizzard?"

Becky's eyes narrowed. Through gritted teeth she managed, "Let me find that out for you, ma'am," before ducking into the back.

Becky didn't suffer fools gladly. After a waiter at the local diner got Becky's order wrong for the third time, she embarked on a mission to get him fired. "I'm not doing it because of a personal vendetta," Becky insisted. "I'm doing it for all the other innocent South Windsorians like myself who specifically requested the sweet potato disco fries with gravy on the side, not normal disco fries drenched in the stuff. What's so hard to understand about that?" Becky pursued her mission by calling the diner daily under the guises of different dissatisfied customers and complaining about the waiter until he was finally let go.

A few moments later, Becky returned to the window. "Ninety-two grams of carbs per ten and a half ounces is based on the Oreo flavor. The Cookie Dough has one hundred and three per serving."

"Well, I'm glad I asked now, aren't I? How many ounces in a medium Oreo Blizzard?"

"Thirteen, so that comes to one hundred and seventeen grams of carbs."

"One hundred and seventeen! Why didn't you just tell me that? If I got one of your Blizzards, I wouldn't have any carbs left for the rest of the week." Alek wondered if this woman and his mother had attended the same difficult customer course.

"Would you like to try some of our delicious low-carb frozen yogurt?"

"No, thank you." The woman snapped her purse closed.

"What! You've blabbered for half an hour and you're not even going to buy anything?"

"Excuse me, young lady, but you really shouldn't speak to customers that way," the woman huffed.

"Well, since you're not buying anything, you're not really a customer, are you?" Becky shot back.

Alek waited for the woman to retreat before he approached the window. "Can you tell me how many carbs there are in two-thirds of a traditional thirteen-ounce Dairy Queen Oreo Cookie Blizzard?"

Becky looked up sharply. Strands of her hair had fallen out of her red paper DQ hat, and a smudge of fudge was smeared across her right cheek.

"Alek, what the hell are you doing here?"

"I just wanted to execute my God-given American right to achieve obesity."

"You must find it hilarious to see me in my stupid uniform."

"It's certainly a nice perk."

"I'll show you a nice perk. Now get out of here before you get me in trouble."

"Becky, please. I need to talk to you."

"It's that easy? You disappear for a week, then just show up here and say that you need to talk to me?" Becky hissed.

"You kicked me out! You're the one who should've called me," Alek protested.

"Look, when you miss someone enough, it doesn't matter who should've called who. You just do it."

"Well, this is what I'm doing, Becky. I'm making first contact. It's your play now."

A thick-limbed woman lumbered up to the service window from behind. "Becky, you know what the policy about friends visiting you at work is." Alek didn't need Becky to tell him that this was Laurie, her infamous manager. The red DQ hat barely fit on her gargantuan head, and her small, beady eyes stared at Becky accusingly.

"You know what, Laurie, I think I'm going to take my break now, okay?"

"But I need help filling up the Arctic Rush machine."

"Laurie, I have three breaks saved up today," Becky continued, the hatred in her voice simmering.

"You'll take your breaks when we have nothing else to do," Laurie insisted smugly.

Becky took the red DQ paper hat off her head. Then, slowly

ripping it into little pieces, she addressed Laurie. "I can forgive you for many things, Laurie. The way you need to take the scrap of power you get being a manager at a Dairy Queen and use it to torture all us hapless innocent employees. Your obvious lack of social graces and the way you envy other people's friends because you don't have any. I can even forgive the slurping sound you make when you try to get the last drops of a milk shake out of the container. All those things I can forgive. But it will take me years—do you hear me?—*years* to be able to have ice cream again without thinking of you. This association will destroy one of the world's greatest gifts." She threw the red scraps that used to be her red DQ hat on the floor at Laurie's feet. "That, I will never forgive."

9

"SO WHAT DO YOU WANT TO TALK ABOUT?" BECKY demanded.

"Well, what if you know somebody who—"

"Enough of the hypotheticals, Alek. That's what got us in trouble last time, remember?"

For the first time Alek could recall, Becky wasn't complaining about having to skate alongside him slowly. She looped him lazily as they made their way home along the highway shoulder.

Then, abruptly, she stopped in front of Alek. Even on her blades, she barely reached his chin. She put her hands on his shoulders and looked him directly in the eye.

"Tell me what you really want to know."

"There's this guy."

"Who?"

"Ethan Novick."

"Ethan Novick of food-fight fame?" Becky asked.

Alek nodded yes. He told her everything, from Ethan's saving him behind the tunnel to the surprise New York adventure yesterday.

"So you just wanted to brag about the new friend you've made?"

"No, Becky, there's more."

He worked his way up to what had happened earlier that day with Ethan in front of the ice cream machine.

"So I walked up to him and . . ."

"And what?" she asked urgently.

"You know what? Never mind."

"You bore me stupid with backstory and you're not going to give me the ending?"

Alek stopped walking. "I'm sorry you think my story is stupid."

"I was just kidding." Becky held out her hand and steadied herself against him. "Just tell me what happened. You know I want to hear. I'm your best friend."

Becky had never used that term before. It didn't surprise Alek necessarily, but invoking the actual title was a commitment. A friend was someone you talked to in school, joined a club with, or who went to your church. A stupid fight in a basement could end a normal friendship. But a best friend was someone you could trust with your life, someone who you knew would be there for you. Being best friends was a promise to work through things no matter what. And why couldn't a best friend be a girl?

Alek and Becky reached the intersection of Etra and Orchard.

"I can go down the rest of the way by myself," she said.

"But I haven't finished telling you what happened with Ethan!"

"You dumb-ass!" Becky screamed. " 'I can go down the rest

of the way by myself' is what I always say when we reach this point in our walk. We go, like, seven days without talking and you've already forgotten."

"Say it again."

"What?"

"Say it again."

"This is stupid."

"Just do it," Alek insisted. He didn't know why, but he knew that if he could get Becky to play along, everything would be fine.

"I can go down the rest of the way by myself," Becky repeated flatly.

"Why don't I walk you to your door? You know how dangerous South Windsor can be on a weekday afternoon," Alek recited.

"That would be lovely, Alek." Becky said it almost as playfully as she usually did.

Alek filled her in on the rest on the way to her house. As humiliating as it was, he even included the heckling from the other Dropouts, because Alek decided that best friends could tell each other about their most embarrassing moments. They reached her front door as Alek finished the rest of the story.

"So what do you think?"

"I think you like him."

"Of course I do. He's so cool."

"No, Alek, I mean I think you *like* him like him."

Alek stopped. "You think I what?"

Becky opened her front door without responding.

"Becky, what do you mean?" Alek pursued her into her house.

"Yes, Becky, whatever do you mean?" Becky's mother's voice echoed from inside.

Alek walked through Becky's front door and into her living room. Becky was popping off her Rollerblades, and she had already managed to open a Diet Dr Pepper. Her parents were sitting on the backless yellow Dutch sofa.

"Alek, we haven't seen you . . ."

". . . in forever. Welcome back."

"Hello, Mr. and Mrs. Boyce."

The Boyces were older than Alek's parents. Still dressed in their white lab coats, they sat in the living room sipping tea under the Ivorian tablecloth hanging above them.

"Alek, help yourself to anything you'd like . . ."

". . . in the kitchen. You know where everything is."

Age wasn't the only difference between the Khederians and the Boyces. Alek's parents would never let a guest just help himself. They would tell the guest what options were available, ask him which he preferred, and either serve him themselves or have Alek do it. Alek remembered his mother making him practice when he was barely in elementary school.

"Alek, you forgot to ask me if I wanted ice in my water," his mother gently reprimanded him during their first session. Both he and Nik had to learn the difference between a water glass (tall) and a juice glass (short) as soon as they were old enough to drink from one.

"You never serve fruit juice with ice, because it's always chilled. And you never serve water in a cup or mug—water is always served in a glass. With water, you have to ask if they want bubbly or flat, room temperature or chilled, and with or without ice."

The Khederians always kept one bottle of sparkling water in the refrigerator and another in the pantry just in case a guest happened to drop by, even after his father got laid off. But Becky's home, like most of *these American* households, was much chiller than that.

"Thank you, Mr. and Mrs. Boyce," Alek said.

Alek wanted to be alone with Becky so he could ask her what she meant about him liking Ethan, but he hadn't seen the Boyces since they had returned from the Geneva conference, and it would've been rude to run down to the basement. So instead he helped himself to some cranberry juice, walked back into the living room, and sat down opposite them on an overstuffed chair, his feet dangling just above the floor. "How was your trip?"

"Just exhilarating, thank you for asking."

"We got to see some . . ."

". . . great friends at the conference . . ."

". . . and catch up on their research at the same time."

"Two birds, one stone."

Since Alek had met them, the Boyces had finished each other's sentences. Alek didn't think he'd ever even seen them apart. His own parents had always divided their responsibilities, even if the nature of that division had changed since his mom started working. Alek's mom might pick up groceries on the way back from work, and his dad would then cook dinner. But the Boyces would go to the grocery store together, then prepare the actual meal, and finally clean up and do the dishes together as well. He always saw Mr. Boyce in the passenger seat when Mrs. Boyce came to pick Becky up, and vice versa.

"Alek, look at . . ."

". . . what we brought back from Geneva. It's cast in the same mold as . . ."

". . . the famous eighteenth-century model."

The Boyces proudly produced a brass bell so large that Alek wondered how they had managed to carry it through the airport and into their home.

"Next time they want to get me up for school, they're going to sneak into my room and gong it right next to my innocent sleeping head," Becky said.

"Now, now, Rebecca . . ."

". . . you know we'd never do that."

"I know, I know! I was making a *joke*, guys." Alek had never figured out how Becky ended up with her sense of humor when her parents took everything literally.

"Listen to us . . ."

". . . rattling on like this. You young people . . ."

". . . probably want to go to the basement and watch movies instead of . . ."

". . . listening to two old fuddy-duddies going on and on about bells."

"Becky, honey, we're going to go . . ."

". . . to visit some friends in Baltimore this weekend. We'll leave you . . ."

". . . the number of where we're staying and some money."

"Great to see you again, Alek, and please . . ."

". . . send our best to your parents."

Becky grabbed another Diet Dr Pepper, having already depleted her first, and Alek followed her downstairs to the basement.

"Your parents are awesome, Becky."

"What do you mean?"

"They're just so the total opposite of mine."

"I guess. But I'd give anything to have that homemade food around. You know, the first number I knew by heart was Scotto's Pizzeria."

Alek and Becky assumed their familiar places on the basement sofa in slightly awkward silence.

"Weren't you telling me about that guy you like?" Becky asked.

"I didn't say I liked him!"

"Alek, that's why you overreacted in the cafeteria today. All Ethan did was ask to chill later. You have no idea what's going on with him. You barely know the guy."

"But—"

"I'm not done. This is the good part." Becky paused for a second and took a deep, long swig of her Diet Dr Pepper. "This is why I know I'm right, because I know what it's like to overreact when you have a crush on someone." Becky paused again, just long enough to make her point. "Do you understand what I'm saying? Because I'd rather save us both the embarrassment of conjuring up the moment of me thrusting myself at you like a woman of the night, okay?"

"I do, Becky. But I know what it's like to have a crush. I remember what it felt like when I asked Gail out the first time, or when I danced with Linsay at the Spring Fling last year."

"And what were your two forays into the dating world like?"

"You know—sweaty palms, knots in my stomach, tongue-tied. Everything they talk about in movies. That's not what I feel like when I talk to Ethan. And whatever I do feel, it's not because I have a crush on him—it's because he's a junior and a D.O. and the kind of guy who starts an epic food fight."

"So, are you saying you don't feel that way around him, or you do?"

"I'm saying . . ." Alek started, then stopped himself. "I'm saying, I really missed you, Becky. It's good to be here with you."

"That's not what I'm talking about, dumb-ass."

"Becky, I think I'd know if I was gay," Alek insisted. "Now, can we talk about something else?"

"So you're saying you're not?" Becky persisted.

"Look, just because I didn't want to kiss you back doesn't mean I like boys," Alek shot back.

Becky put her soda down and stood up. "Listen, it's really good to talk to you and I've missed you, too, and I haven't had anyone to see movies with and even if Mandy and Suzie were around I like you more than them, but if you say stupid things like that, you can just get out of here right now, understand?"

Alek jerked around, surprised by Becky's outburst, and accidentally knocked over his soda.

"You dumb-ass." Becky ran to the bathroom and returned with some slightly damp paper towels. "Now remember, dab gently to lift the stain instead of stamping it in."

"Thanks, Martha Stewart."

Alek crumpled the paper towels into little balls, dabbed them until the stain went away, and tossed them into the wastebasket. "I'm sorry, Becky."

"Okay then." Becky sat back down and, just like that, everything was okay again.

"I guess what I mean is I just don't think about guys that

way. I don't know what else to say. I mean, I'm fourteen years old. Don't you think that if I was gay I'd know by now?"

"I don't know. One of my uncles didn't come out until he was fortysomething. He was already married and had kids. I loved having Thanksgiving with him. My uncle, his ex-wife, his new partner, his ex-wife's second husband, the kids from the first marriage, and the stepkids from his ex-wife's second marriage. That family tree branched out all over the place."

"Well, these days no one waits until they're that old to come out."

"All I'm saying is that it sounds to me like you have a crush on Ethan. I don't even know if that means you're gay."

Alek looked away from Becky. The possibility that he was gay had never occurred to him. He had enjoyed kissing the girlfriends he'd had in middle school. He never checked out girls the way that some of the other guys his age did, but he had been brought up with better manners than that. And he never thought about guys that way when he was changing in the locker room for gym.

"Becky, if I were gay, and I'm not saying that I am, but if I were, would you still want to be my best friend?" Asking Becky that question directly took all the courage that Alek had been able to muster.

"Are you serious?"

"Very."

"Alek, not to be harsh, but I don't care if you're gay or not. Nobody does." Alek started to say something, but Becky continued, not giving him a chance to respond. "Because anyone who thinks there is something wrong with being gay is like those

106

people you read about in History who believed in segregation. But I bet you Ethan cares, because it sounds to me like he has a crush on you, too."

"Becky, you're a great best friend."

"And you're a cornball. Apologize to Ethan. Since you apologized to me, there's no reason you can't apologize to him. I'm much more intimidating than he is."

10

"*NO* ONE GETS TO CHURCH ON TIME," ALEK INSISTED through a yawn as the Khederians scrambled their way through the chaotic Sunday morning ritual of trying to get out of the house. It figured that the one way his parents chose to defy Armenian tradition was by insisting on punctuality. "Last week, the Hagopians didn't even show up until we'd been there for two hours. Two hours! "

"It's important to me to set a good example," his mother insisted.

An example to whom? Alek wanted to ask, but decided against risking it.

In spite of the plans, preparations, and calculations that were made each Saturday night, it always felt like the universe conspired to set a series of events into motion that would prevent the Khederians from leaving the house the following morning with the ninety minutes needed to make the trip to church comfortably. This morning, for example, every time Alek went to use the bathroom, Nik was already using it. In addition, and equally inexplicably, he spent fifteen minutes looking for the jacket and tie he'd set aside the night before, finally finding they'd somehow made their way to the basement.

And when the universe wasn't getting in his way, his parents were. Inevitably, just as the family was ready to leave, his parents would remember something that absolutely *needed* to get done before they could depart. Today, they chose sweeping the garage.

"Are you done, boys?" his father called out. Alek knelt down, holding the dustpan as far away from himself as possible, while Nik swept the dirt in his direction.

"You're getting me dirty on purpose!"

"Am not—you just don't know how to hold it," Nik protested.

"I'm sorry, Honor-Track-older-brother-of-mine. Please, show me the right way to hold a dustpan."

Nik dropped the broom and grabbed the dustpan out of Alek's hands. "See, you want to hold it up at an angle, like this," he instructed.

"That's what I was doing. And this is what you were doing." Alek demonstrated, using the broom to kick the dirt at Nik.

"Mom, Alek's making a mess!" Nik said as their mother entered the garage.

"Aleksander, don't dirty your brother's clothes! We're already late!" She clasped a single strand of pearls around her neck and squinted at her watch anxiously.

"We're only late because you're making us clean the garage!" Alek cried. "I still don't understand why this couldn't wait until we get back!"

"Well, God forbid something happened to us and people had to come into our home—what would they think if they found a dirty garage?"

"Let me great this straight," Alek said. "If—God forbid—we were kidnapped or got into a terrible car accident, something so terrible that people had to forcibly enter our home, the thing you're concerned about is the cleanliness of our garage? In that scenario, I *hope* that's the worst thing we have to think about."

"Why are you always so morbid, Alek?" his mother asked.

"Seriously," Nik chimed in. "Have you thought about therapy?" Nik turned around and spoke to their mother. "It's okay, Mom—I can finish up here by myself."

"Thanks, honey, I know I can always count on you." Then she turned to Alek. "You can help me look for the car keys."

Alek rolled his eyes in what he wished was surprise. The final act of the Sunday morning departure ritual was that his parents would misplace something they couldn't leave without.

"But you guys have *three* copies! You can't find any of them?"

"Well, I know I lost a pair when my handbag was stolen last month," his mother recalled.

"It wasn't stolen. You left it in the cart at Whole Foods."

"Well, yes, but nobody turned it in to the lost and found, right? That means it was stolen."

Alek put his head in his hands. "Well, what about the spare set?"

"We gave those to the Eisingers in case of an emergency."

"So why don't I just run over and get them?"

"Honey, do you know how early it is? On a Sunday? I'd hate to disturb them."

Alek contemplated calling his mother's attention to the ridiculousness of asking neighbors to hold on to keys in the event of an emergency and then deciding not to claim them in an actual emergency, but decided on a more practical tactic.

"What about Dad's keys?"

"Well, I'm sure I put them right here when I came in last night," his father said, inspecting the empty bowl on the semicircular table just inside the Khederians' front door.

"Did you retrace your steps after you came in?" his mother asked.

"That's a good idea, honey! Let's see, I came in, took off my shoes, then went to the bathroom," Alek's father said, re-creating each incident as he was describing it. "Then I washed my hands, went to the basement—no, wait—the kitchen first—and poured myself a glass of water. Or was it Pellegrino?"

"I don't think you actually need to narrate *every* detail," Alek said through clenched teeth. "Just see if the keys somehow ended up somewhere else."

"Now you've broken my concentration and I'm going to need to start again," his father said. He walked back to the front door. "I came in last night, took off my shoes, and then went to the bathroom. After that I went to the basement—wait—no—the kitchen, and then—"

"I found the keys—they're in the car," Nik yelled from the garage.

"Yes! That's it! I must've left them in the car!" Alek's father exclaimed. They filed into the garage, and Alek silently prayed thanks that Nik didn't ask to drive. His brother wasn't a bad driver, but the way their mother clenched her knuckles as if she were on a roller coaster whenever Nik practiced with his permit increased everybody's stress level.

A few miles later, right before they were about to turn onto the highway, his mother asked, "Did someone remember to bring the tabbouleh?" They collectively groaned and, a sharp U-turn later, were heading back home to pick up the bulgur wheat/parsley/tomato salad that his dad had prepared the night before for the potluck following services.

And they were back on the road, the Tupperware of tabbouleh sitting on Alek's lap because their father was worried that it would spill in the trunk. Alek had given up pointing out that the plastic container could safely hold liquid when it was properly sealed.

Alek looked at the car clock. The seven forty-five seemed to be mocking him, because he knew instead of just showing up late like everyone else, his father would insist on speeding to try to make up the lost time. Alek just prayed they didn't get pulled over like they did last year. Seeing his mother coerce, beg, and threaten her way out of the ticket was fun, but he'd rather not risk an encounter with the law again.

They arrived at the church just as the service was starting and sprinted into the cathedral, handing the tabbouleh off to a volunteer like a baton in an Olympic relay. Alek had to employ his entire arsenal of activities and mental exercises to keep himself awake during the service. First, he counted the number of people in attendance—this Sunday, 157 Armenians and their loved ones had woken up early to make the nine a.m. service. Or rather, that's how many people were sitting in the pews by the end. Just as Alek had predicted, most of them trickled in sometime over the course of the next hour.

Next, he started naming all of the scenes depicted in the stained glass windows: the archangels, the Holy Family, the Ascension. Last, he came to the patron saint of the church, Saint Stephen, the first Christian martyr, who allegedly prayed to Christ to forgive his murderers as they were stoning him to death. Alek's eyes lingered on Saint Stephen, hoping that Ethan would be as kind to him tomorrow as Saint Stephen had been to his killers. After all, freaking out in a cafeteria had to be a lesser offense than stoning someone to death. Even if after that freak-out, you sat next to the person in Algebra for two days wanting—but not finding—the courage to apologize. Right?

Alek watched the priests walk up and down the aisles, swinging metal globes filled with smoky incense attached to rods on chains. Every time, Alek hoped that one of the chains would snap, sending the metal orbs and burning incense all over the congregation. He didn't want the cathedral set ablaze, but he did think it would provide a welcome distraction.

The priest was finally wending his way to the communion, which would be followed by the sermon. After the sermon had been delivered in Armenian, the priest would repeat it in English so all the faux Armenians like Alek who couldn't understand Armenian could still benefit from the wise words. Nik always made a point of reacting to the first delivery of the service, so the whole congregation could see he understood Armenian. Sometimes Alek would react along, nodding knowingly with the adults or looking solemn for a certain passage, just to irritate Nik.

Two and a half hours later the service finally ended, and the families filed out of the cathedral and into the potluck line. When the weather permitted, like today, they sat outdoors on the great lawn behind the church. This time was also used to keep the congregation abreast of various church-related organizations, like Saturday and Sunday school, Armenian conversation and Bible studies classes, and the Armenian Church Youth Organization of America (ACYOA) chapter, of which Nik was, predictably, an active member. Alek dreaded the day his parents forced him to join one of the church youth groups.

The Khederians were one of the last families to get to the potluck, since Alek's mother liked to sit up front for the service. By the time they reached their tabbouleh dish on the food table, it was almost gone. Alek could see his father smile proudly, especially because a neighboring tabbouleh dish had remained untouched. After piling their plates with lamb, pastries, yogurt, and salad, the Khederians joined Nik's girlfriend's parents, the Hovanians, at a large round table.

"Do you want any more lemonade?" Nik asked Nanar before he sat down.

"No, thank you," Nanar replied formally.

Alek had never been able to get a read on Nik's girlfriend. She was almost as tall as Nik, but curvy where he was beanpole straight, with the prerequisite dark brown Armenian hair and eyes. Although she was just a few months older than Nik, she almost looked like a woman, while Nik still straddled that awkward space between being a boy and a man. The only thing that Alek could tell she and Nik had in common, besides being Armenian, was wanting to please their parents.

"Are you sure?" Nik asked her again.

"Yes, I'm sure. Thank you, Andranik," Nanar replied.

Nik sat down next to his girlfriend. But instead of immediately digging into his food, he took a moment, looked at her, and smiled. Nanar smiled back and put her hand on his. The entire exchange only took a few seconds, but reminded Alek how much more Nik smiled when he was around Nanar.

Mrs. Hovanian took a bite of her bureg, a savory pastry triangle, and started coughing violently. She was a plump woman, shorter and darker than most Armenians, with a pronounced nose and bright red cheeks. For a moment, Alek thought she was going to commit the unpardonable Armenian sin of spitting out food, but she managed to swallow it down with a large gulp of water.

"Are you okay?" Alek's mother asked her.

"*I'm* okay. But I wish I could say the same of the Kirikians' buregs," she complained, folding the rest of the pastry into a napkin. "They're so dry. I guess that's what happens when you bring in a Macedonian woman to make them and you pretend that you made them yourself. You think any of us would make buregs this dry?"

"Of course not, dear," Mr. Hovanian, a tall, prematurely balding man, agreed. "Isn't that right, Nanar?"

"Yes, Papa," Nanar said quietly.

"I think the Kirikians' buregs are okay," Alek's dad ventured.

Mrs. Hovanian laughed heartily. "That's very kind of you, Boghos, but I can't help but notice you didn't take any."

"Have you tried any of the sarma?" Alek's mom asked.

"We'd like to, but it's all stuffed cabbage," Mrs. Hovanian

complained. "Not a grape leaf to be seen. I was hoping for some dolma as well, but all the stuffed peppers were gone by the time I reached the table, and I decided against the zucchini, since I find the summer squashes too stringy. But of course we love your tabbouleh, Kadarine. Nanar, tell Mrs. Khederian how much you like her tabbouleh."

"It's always the perfect ratio of bulgur to parsley to vegetables, Mrs. Khederian," Nanar responded on cue.

"It's a family recipe." Alek's mom beamed in response.

"Boghos, Kadarine, would you excuse us for a moment?" Mrs. Hovanian said, getting up. Her husband and daughter followed her. "We'd like to ask the Kalfayans about carpooling for the vacation. And please, no one mention the kufteh they made for last year's trip. The beef was so overspiced, I was sick for the whole vacation!"

Alek's mother watched them leave. The moment the Hovanians were out of earshot, she said, "Can you imagine how difficult it must be going through life finding fault with everything?"

"That must be very hard for you to imagine," Alek deadpanned. No one in his family, however, noted the irony.

The Hovanians returned a few moments later, beaming. "The Kalfayans will be renting a minivan, so we can get a ride up with them to Niagara Falls," Mr. Hovanian reported happily.

Nanar turned to Alek. "I was so sorry to hear you won't be able to come on the vacation, Alek. I was looking forward to spending more time with you."

Alek was touched by Nanar's sincerity. "Nanar, please don't worry about it."

"And Mom and Dad are letting Alek choose next year's vacation," Nik said. Alek waited for the insult or cut-down to follow, but instead, Nik continued eating his bureg. Nanar's kindness apparently transformed Nik into a normal human being.

"Mom, Dad, just make sure you leave the number for your hotel so that I can get in touch with you in case anything comes up and you're out of range." Alek stabbed a strip of lamb with his fork and shoved it into his mouth.

"We'll make sure to leave all of that information with the sitter," his mom assured him.

"What sitter?" Alek smiled back at his mom.

Alek's mom looked confused. "What do you mean, dear?" she asked, trying to keep up appearances for the Hovanians' sake.

"Well, Becky's parents have been leaving her alone since she was thirteen."

"But that's just for a weekend—this is for a full week."

"It's not really a full week. You're leaving Tuesday and coming back on Sunday, so that's only five days, really. Besides, I'm *fourteen*! Are you saying I can't take care of myself?"

"Alek," his father began, "why don't we talk about this later?"

Alek knew this meant, *There's no way we're going to let you have your way, but since we don't want to appear tyrannical in front of the Hovanians, we'll just wait to tell you no when we're in private.*

"You know, Papa started taking Mama on his business trips when I turned fourteen," Nanar offered.

Alek looked at Nanar with gratitude for resuscitating his chance for a few days of freedom.

"Really?" Alek's mom smiled weakly.

"I think it's really good for kids to have some independence. It helps them grow up," Mr. Hovanian explained. "Besides, with e-mail and cell phones and Facebook—"

"You have a Facebook account, Mr. Hovanian?" Alek asked.

"Of course he does. We both do!" Mrs. Hovanian confirmed. "How else do you think we keep up with the AGBU and the United Armenian Fund?"

"With all of this technology, keeping track of your kids has never been easier. Even when you're away," Mr. Hovanian finished up.

"And if anything did happen, I could just run over to the Eisingers," Alek added. "As long as it's not too early—I'd hate to inconvenience them for an emergency." Alek admonished himself immediately for taking the jab before he'd clinched the deal, but he couldn't help himself.

"I guess if we gave you a list of rules that you'd have to follow or be grounded for the rest of your natural life, and you made sure to check in every day, and night, it might work," Alek's mom conceded.

Alek looked over at Nik. This is exactly the time when he'd usually say something to spoil things. As expected, Nik opened his mouth to speak.

"Oh, Mom, relax. He'll be fine," Nik said.

Alek stared at his brother, dumbfounded. But Nik just continued to eat and stare into Nanar's eyes.

Alek's mom looked at his dad for approval. When he nodded, she said, "No more than one friend over at a time, bed by eleven, no more than one hour of television on school days—"

"Wow! A whole hour! You guys are getting soft in your old age."

His mom ignored Alek's jab. "And you call every day . . ."

". . . at least once," his dad added.

". . . *at least* once to tell us everything is okay."

"Deal."

The eerie orange light flickered, daring Alek to enter. He vividly recalled Jack shoving and mounting him the last time he had dared to go to the other side. But he had promised himself that he would apologize to Ethan today, and since he'd failed to do it during Algebra, he had no option but to brave the tunnel, Jack, and the rest of the Dropouts.

Alek took one step, then another. When he was halfway through, the lights blinked out, stranding him in darkness. Alek forced himself to continue stepping forward, keeping his focus on the promise of light at the end.

When he finally emerged, he saw the D.O.s skating, flipping, and skidding through the parking lot they'd claimed. Before he could locate Ethan, he heard Jack's voice boom across the parking lot. "What're you doing here, dumb-ass?"

"Screw you, asshole," Alek responded without missing a beat.

"Nice," Alek heard a voice offer. He turned around and saw Ethan hovering on his board, lazily circling a traffic cone. "I thought I was going to have to bail your ass out of this one, just like last time."

"You're not going to have to save me anymore, Ethan."

"Is that because I'm going to be too busy going to hell?"

"Look." Alek took a deep breath. He found himself wanting to look at anything but Ethan—the untied lace on his left shoe, a guy with a baseball cap on backward retaping the top of his skateboard—but he forced himself to make eye contact. "I'm really sorry about that."

"You better be."

"I am." He wished he could be alone with Ethan, but if this was where the apology was going to have to happen, so be it. "I think I did some serious overreacting."

"No shit!"

"I just thought—"

"You made what you thought pretty clear that day. You thought that I was embarrassed to be seen with you in front of my friends. Well, let me tell you something, *dude*. Every one of those guys, even the ones who can be total assholes like Jack, accept me for who I am. I'm not saying they threw me a parade when I came out, but they don't care about my being gay. Which I think is pretty awesome, especially considering that none of them are. So they were just having some fun that day. Everything else was your own shit."

Ethan's words stung Alek, but not because they weren't true. He swallowed his response, and his pride. "That's why I'm here now, Ethan. 'Cause I know I acted like a jerk. So I came to say I'm sorry. Here." Alek pulled a package out of his JanSport backpack and handed it to Ethan.

"What's that?"

"I think apologies are easy. You just say 'I'm sorry' and expect everything to be fine. Gifts are better. They say 'I'm sorry, and

I'm willing to spend a few bucks and some time and effort to show you how sorry I really am.'"

"Nice, Polly-O." Ethan nodded his head in approval.

"Well, open it already!"

Ethan sat down on his skateboard with his back to Alek and ripped open the package. When the wrapping paper lay on the ground in shreds, Ethan held up the contents. "A book?" he said.

"Flip through it," Alek instructed. Ethan did, and Alek continued talking. "You remember how, when you used to buy CDs, they came with these great little books that had all the lyrics? Well, I made a little booklet of all the Rufus lyrics. I put them by album, so it starts with *Rufus Wainwright*, and then come *Poses*, *Want One* and *Two*, *Release the Stars*, *All Days Are Nights*, and then *Out of the Game*." Ethan didn't say anything, so Alek continued. "I'm sure you already know most of the words, but I just thought it would be nice to have them all printed out together, you know."

Alek hoped this would at least get some kind of reaction from Ethan, but he still didn't say anything. After a few more moments of silence, Alek added, "I hope you don't think this is stupid, but I didn't really know what else to get you. I mean, I don't know anything about skateboarding or . . ."

Ethan's shoulders started heaving. Alek took two steps backward.

"You know, if you don't want it, I can take it back," Alek offered huffily. Putting himself on the line was one thing, but there was no way he was going to let Ethan laugh at him for the peace offering that he had spent most of the weekend putting together.

Ethan turned around to look at Alek, and Alek saw tears running down his face.

"Come with me," Ethan said. Without waiting for a response, Ethan got on his skateboard and began to skate away. "I'll see you guys later," he called over his shoulder, wiping his nose with the back of his hand.

"Later, Ethan," Jack called back.

"See you tomorrow," a spiky-haired guy yelled.

Ethan turned around. "What're you waiting for?" he asked Alek, who had been standing frozen like a Rodin statue. Alek grabbed his backpack and ran after the boy on the skateboard.

11

ETHAN JUMPED OFF HIS SKATEBOARD AND UNLOCKED
the front door to an attached brown row house with a key hanging on one of his many pocket chains. He wove through the piles
of books, records, CDs, DVDs, magazines, and newspapers
stacked on the shelves, in every corner, and against every available
wall surface. It was hard to make out what kind of furniture was
in the house because everything was drowning in piles.

"My father likes things," Ethan offered wryly, answering Alek's
unasked question.

"What does he do with all of this?" Alek exclaimed, gestur-
ing to the books and CDs and DVDs.

"He's read or listened to or watched every book, album, or
DVD in this house."

"Are you kidding me?"

But Ethan was on the move again.

Alek followed Ethan into his room, thinking how terrifying this setting would've been just a few weeks ago.

"Close the door," Ethan said over his shoulder. Every wall in Ethan's room was covered with images, making Alek feel like he'd stepped into a kaleidoscope. Even the ceiling was plastered with pictures.

From underneath his bed, Ethan pulled out a medium-size green plastic bin. As he started to work his way through the contents, Alek tried to decipher the magazine cutouts, posters, and printouts staring at him.

All of the images were of men. Some were movie stars, like Ryan Gosling, Bradley Cooper, Jude Law, and Johnny Depp. Some were athletes: Alek recognized Tom Brady, Drew Brees, Aaron Rodgers, Rafael Nadal, Dwayne Wade, and Joe Mauer. And some, Alek realized, were gay celebrities, like Anderson Cooper, Neil Patrick Harris, and Alan Cumming.

Then there was an entire wall dedicated entirely to models at various points of undress. Alek guessed that he saw more semi-nude men in Ethan's room than he had seen in his life cumulatively. He couldn't find one totally frontally naked man, but many of the men were naked from the waist up, and some of them were entirely naked but photographed from behind. Finding himself blushing, Alek refocused on Ethan, who finally found what he was looking for. He slid the green plastic bin back under the bed and turned to Alek.

"Look at this."

Alek stared at the booklet, dumbstruck. It contained the lyrics to all the Rufus songs, organized by albums, almost identical to the one Alek had given Ethan.

"I've been racking my brain, thinking about every conversation you and I have had," Ethan said. "And I'm sure I didn't mention that I had this. So I can only conclude that it's pure coincidence that you made it for me. And that's freaky, man."

"Why? I'm sure that lots of people know you love Rufus."

"This wasn't given to me by just anyone. It was a gift. From my ex-boyfriend."

Ethan's gaze went to a framed portrait on his desk of him with his arm around a handsome, tall guy with a solid jaw and curly blond hair.

"Is that him?"

"That's Remi."

"Why'd you guys break up?"

"Long story."

"If you don't want to tell me you don't have to, Ethan, but I wish you would."

"It's not that I don't want to, it's just . . . well, it's embarrassing."

"More embarrassing than telling someone to go to hell?"

Ethan laughed in spite of himself. "Well, not that embarrassing. Nothing would be *that* embarrassing."

"So what're you waiting for?"

Ethan hopped on his bed and lay down on his stomach. Alek sat on the floor next to the bed, looking up at him.

"Well, Remi was one of my dad's students at NYU. He came here from Australia. My dad thought he was mad smart, but that his papers weren't up to par. So he told Remi to stay after class one day and asked him what was going on. Turned out Remi could barely work on school because his life was falling apart."

"What do you mean?"

"Well, his folks lost all their money right before he started school, so he had to hold down all of these jobs and barely had time to do his homework. He couldn't afford student housing, so he was sofa-cruising from one friend's apartment to another. My father freaked when he found out that Remi had spent some nights on the street, so he told him to stay in our guest room until he found a regular habitat. I think it was only supposed to be temporary, but by the time spring semester rolled around, Remi was still here. My dad liked having him around, and he did all the shit that my dad hated, like dishes and laundry and vacuuming. And of course I didn't mind because by that point we were pretty serious."

"But he must have been way older than you."

"Not really. He skipped a grade, so he was only seventeen, and I'd just turned fifteen. It wasn't that big of a deal. And look at him." Ethan handed the portrait on the desk to Alek. "He was the kind of guy that turned heads."

"Did your dad freak out when he found out you two were together?"

"I don't know if he ever knew, honestly. Most of the time, I think he's totally clueless. I guess he thought Remi would be a good influence, like the older brother I never had, and in a lot of ways he was. Remi turned me on to Rufus, and although I had hung out a lot in the city before I met him, he had a knack for finding cool people and places. He always said that if he were stranded in the desert he wouldn't survive a day, but in a city he knew how to get by. He's the one who taught me the bathroom train trick and how to do the city on ten bucks for the day—"

"Hey, that reminds me. I still had five bucks left over."

"That's because I decided to skip the last part."

"Why?"

"Because you were being a salty bitch. It'll just have to wait for the next time we get to the city."

Alek inhaled sharply. His mind started racing with the possibilities of what another day in New York with Ethan could entail.

"Now where was I?" Ethan sat up. "That's right. Remi knew just how to navigate his way through the city. Wait until I show you his Barnes & Noble trick, or his umbrella special."

"What does that mean?" Alek sat up eagerly.

"I told you, you'll have to wait and see," Ethan said playfully, leaning forward for extra emphasis. Alek scooted back slightly, stretching his legs out.

"I know this may sound stupid," Ethan continued, "but I thought I was going to spend the rest of my life with him. From the moment we met, everything felt so right."

"Well, he sounds just about perfect," Alek said.

"He was," Ethan replied. "I guess."

"You guess?"

"Well, it's just that sometimes . . ." He trailed off, looking away.

"What, Ethan?"

"Sometimes he did things that really upset me. But I knew it was just me being immature."

"Like what?"

"Well, some nights, he just wouldn't come home. I'd wait up until two or three for him, and nothing—not a text or call or anything. And whenever I asked him where he'd been, he'd say he was studying late at a friend's place. But then the next day we'd be chilling with one of his friends, who'd let it slip that they'd been out clubbing the night before. You know—shady shit like that. And, like, I didn't really care. I mean, he was in college and he could do whatever he wanted. But I just wished he wouldn't lie to me about it, you know? Especially when I knew he was hooking up with other guys."

"He cheated on you?"

"It wasn't really cheating, because we weren't monogamous."

"Really?"

"Yeah, that's pretty normal in the gay world." Ethan lay back down on his stomach. "I didn't know that until Remi told me. I hated the idea of his being in the city all the time with all that temptation. But Remi said, 'I'm not going to let some American teenager tie me down when I'm in the middle of my sexual prime, regardless of how cute he is,'" Ethan quoted, using an Australian accent. "After he disappeared, I promised myself that I would never date someone again unless it was just the two of us. It was too hard the other way."

"So what happened?"

Ethan didn't respond.

Alek scooched a little closer to Ethan's bed. He said softly, "Tell me, Ethan. Please?"

"Well, one day in the middle of last summer, I woke up and he wasn't here."

"Stayed out all night again?"

"No—he was totally gone. He packed everything up and just disappeared, like he'd never been here. I mean, I knew there was stuff going on with his family back home—he wasn't sure if he'd have enough money for the next semester, and I think his dad was sick. But I never imagined that he'd just vanish on me like that. He was my first everything." Ethan paused for emphasis.

Alek looked at him quizzically.

"My first *everything*," Ethan repeated.

"Oh!" Alek exclaimed.

"I mean, I'd made out with a few guys before him, but that's it. By the time he disappeared, we'd already been together for months. And we were going real strong. At least, I thought we were. And then he was gone. No note, nothing. I asked my dad, and he said, 'Didn't he tell you? Remi bought his return ticket weeks ago.' Something about his having told my dad and not me just slayed me. I ran from the kitchen table up to my room, put Rufus on repeat, and cried all day. I just couldn't believe he would do that to me."

"Did you try to e-mail him or anything like that?"

"Of course! But his NYU account got deactivated, so anything I sent got bounced back to me. And he never responded to the Facebook messages I sent him—not like he ever checked his account anyway—and I didn't have his family's number in Australia. Even now, if somebody wants to disappear, they just can." Ethan took a breath and swallowed deeply. "When I kidnapped you to go into the city last week, that was the one-year anniversary of Remi's departure. I hadn't been to the city since, because it reminded me of him too much. But when I saw that Rufus had been rescheduled to that exact day, I took it as a sign. Honestly, I had such a good time with you that I didn't even think about him, except for a few times at the concert."

"Like during 'Do I Disappoint You'?" Alek asked.

"You noticed?"

Alek nodded.

"That was our song, 'cause every time he'd come home after having stayed out all night, he'd sing it to me and I'd have to forgive him," Ethan said wistfully. "I wish you could've met him, Alek. I think you'd have really liked him."

"I don't," Alek said.

"What?"

"He sounds like a real jerk."

"You've never even met him."

"I don't need to have met him to hear how shitty he treated you."

"You don't get it, Alek. Remi had an effect on people. I saw it happen to my dad, to his friends, to strangers, and it certainly happened to me." Ethan sat up, searching for the right words. "Remi's attention felt like a super-bright spotlight, shining just on you. It was like nothing else in the world existed. Being with him made you feel like you were really living, like every second counted."

"And because of that he could treat you however he wanted to? He waltzes in here, gets you to fall for him, sleeps in your house, eats your food, doesn't make any commitments, and then disappears without a trace. I mean, it wouldn't have killed him to leave you a note, or tell you he was going to go so you could say goodbye to him. And what, they don't have forwarding addresses or phone numbers in Australia?"

"You don't understand, Alek."

"I think I do." Alek was getting worked up now, like he did when he talked about the Armenian Genocide. "You know, my parents are always asking me and Nik to think about what it means to be a man. And they're not talking about turning eighteen. They're talking about taking responsibility and being good to people and owning your actions. Remi might have been sexy and fun and had good taste in music, but I'll tell you, he doesn't sound like a man to me. I mean, look at how he treated you—a year later and you're still hung up on him."

"I always felt like I was just so lucky to be with him," Ethan said.

"Don't you see, Ethan? He was the lucky one."

"You think so?"

"Ethan, look at you—you're, like, the coolest guy at South Windsor, everyone likes you, you dress so cool, and you even ride a skateboard, for God's sake!"

"It's not a skateboard. It's a shortboard."

"Same thing."

"It is not!" Ethan insisted. "Shortboards are better for tricks."

"Okay—you even ride a shortboard! This guy totally took you for granted, because everyone I know would be thrilled to call you his boyfriend."

"You know, when I came home after our day in the city, I just crashed, thinking about Remi and about how much I missed him. And then the next day was worse. And when you walked up to me at that ice cream machine, I just felt myself crumble inside. Around Remi, I felt like I was always trying to act like I was good enough. But around you, I don't want to pretend or hide. That's why I didn't say anything in the cafeteria that day. I knew that in five seconds, I'd be crying on your shoulder."

"That's what it's there for, Ethan."

Alek leaned in, took Ethan's face in his hands, and kissed him.

12

"YOU KISSED HIM!" BECKY SHRIEKED, NEARLY CHOKING on her Diet Dr Pepper.

"Keep your voice down. My parents haven't left yet!" Alek whispered.

Becky and Alek were sitting on the bed in his room. The Tuesday morning sun blasted through his window, hitting a clock shaped like a robot that he'd received as a party favor at a friend's bar mitzvah.

"Sorry," Becky whispered. "But why didn't you tell me earlier?"

"It just happened yesterday. What did you want me to do? Call you from his room?"

"Well, it wouldn't have killed you!" Becky blurted. "I'm your best friend. I have a right to know these things *before* they happen."

"I'll try to remember that."

"Alek, is this the appropriate time to remind you how you were just telling me you're not gay?"

Alek sat in silence for a moment. He could still feel Ethan's lips on his own, a memory that felt like a dream.

"I guess I was wrong," he said simply.

"I knew it. I knew it! That's why you didn't kiss me back. No straight man could resist my charms."

"Honestly, I don't know if I'm *gay*. I mean, I'm not going to say that I'm never going to kiss a girl again. It's just probably less likely—like you ever making another friend."

"I'm going to rise above your sarcasm because this is a very special time for you, and when you look back on it, I want you to remember what a supportive, loving presence I was." Becky jumped up and started pacing around the room, which was as meticulous as the rest of the house. "Don't stop. What happened after?"

"After what?" Alek asked innocently.

"After you kissed him, fool. Did he freak out? Did you freak out? Did you guys go all the way?"

"Are you kidding me? All the way?"

"Just tell me what happened." Becky grabbed the Diet Dr Pepper she had smuggled in for Alek. "And no more drink for you until I know everything."

Alek closed his eyes so he could remember every detail. "You should've seen the look on his face. You know how cool and composed Ethan is? Well, if his eyes got any bigger, they would've met in the middle of his face."

"Was it different? I mean, is kissing a boy different from kissing a girl?"

Alek sat back and searched for the right words. "It was totally the same, and totally different. He hadn't shaved in a few days, and his stubble rubbed against my face. That was different."

"I know some girls who have stubble."

"Becky, do you want me to talk about this or do you want to crack jokes?"

"Talk! Talk! Talk!" She plopped down on the rolling chair at his desk and swiveled around.

"It was rougher. And I don't just mean the stubble. Whenever I've kissed a girl, it's been gentle. And sweet. But there's something about kissing someone who's bigger than you that makes it rougher. Not in a bad way. In a sexy way. You don't have to hold back because you're not scared you're going to hurt them."

"And did you feel like, 'This is it'? Did music swell and fireworks explode and did you think to yourself, 'This is what a kiss is supposed to feel like'?"

"It was like ice cream."

"I worked at DQ. Trust me, it's not like ice cream."

"No, I mean, it's like all my life I've been eating frozen yogurt. And kissing boys is ice cream."

"I can't believe how cool you sound right now."

"Are you making fun of me?"

"No way, Alek." Becky stopped pacing and looked out the window. "You know how you're always blushing? It's one of my favorite things about you. Anything vaguely embarrassing happens, and you go lobster. But you're not even a little pink. I mean pink in the blushing way, not the gay way."

Alek didn't have to look into the mirror to know that Becky was right.

"You're holding out on me." Becky leaped on Alek's bed and continued jumping up and down. "Tell me what else happened."

"Okay, okay! Just calm down." Alek took a breath and waited for Becky to settle down before he continued. "Honestly, we just sat there kissing for a while. I don't know how long, because I lost track of time, like when you're watching a really good movie."

"Like a really good Audrey Hepburn movie or a really good Katharine Hepburn movie?"

"Becky," Alek admonished her.

"Never mind—I know what you mean."

"Well, he got over the shock of my going in for the kiss pretty quickly. And besides being a guy, he's also the first older person I've ever kissed. He really knew what he was doing."

Becky rolled on the bed in excitement, kicking her feet in the air and almost knocking over both Diet Dr Peppers.

"And then?"

"Sometime later, we heard a knock on his door, and I almost jumped up in the air, I was so surprised. Turns out his dad had come home and we were too busy—um—doing things to hear him."

"I'm sure you were."

"So we . . . disengaged, and his father says through the door, 'You in there, Eth?' And Ethan goes, 'Yeah, Dad, with a friend,' in a way that was clearly not an invitation, and his dad goes, 'Well, hope you guys are having fun,' and we almost died laughing. His dad went away, but the moment had sorta passed, you know?"

Alek couldn't believe that Ethan's father hadn't insisted on meeting his guest, the way Alek's parents would've. But then again, the idea of his parents inviting someone to live in their house the way Ethan's dad had invited Remi would never occur to the Khederians. Alek waited until he couldn't hear Ethan's father's footsteps before he spoke.

"You really don't think your dad knew about you and Remi?" Alek had asked Ethan after his father left.

"I don't think so, but honestly, we don't talk about those kinds of things."

"You mean, he'd freak out if he found out you're gay?"

"Look at my room, Alek." Ethan pointed to the cocoon of men's faces, chests, abs, and asses staring back at them. "If you were blind, deaf, dumb, and mute you would still know I'm gay. My dad doesn't care about that. I'm just not close to him in that way. We talk about books, or music, or sports. Not about the personal stuff. And I'm pretty sure he knew Remi was gay when he invited him to live with us. He either didn't put it together or it just didn't matter to him," Ethan had explained. "Now that I think about it, I didn't really have anyone I could talk to about Remi, the way I am now with you."

Alek looked at Becky, realizing how lucky he was to have a friend like her.

"What happened then?" Becky asked.

"We talked for a while, you know, not about anything really, just talked. Then I realized how late it had gotten, so I had to come home." Alek lay down on his back and used a pillow to prop up his head. "I wonder what it'll be like in school tomorrow."

"Very awkward," Becky said. "What're you going to do? Hang out with the D.O.s? Maybe you should practice burping, farting, and smoking so you can blend in."

"I'll do my best."

"It was considerate of you, since you decided to have your first boy-on-boy action on a Monday, to do it the day before July Fourth so you could use the holiday that celebrates this nation's birth to process the experience with your best friend."

"Happy Independence Day," Alek said.

"Right back at you, kiddo. Shouldn't we go to a barbecue or something tonight?"

"I guess," Alek said. "But with my folks leaving today, I'll probably just stay home."

"Well, Alek, I'm really happy for you. Honestly. Remember that gay uncle I told you about who didn't come out until he was already married with kids? Think about all the years he lost. And here you are at fourteen, which is not nearly as old as it sounds, and you've already figured this out about yourself. I mean, you did have your best friend helping you, but still."

Alek waited for a sarcastic comment to undercut Becky's earnestness, but none came. "Thanks, Becky," he said gently.

"Are you going to have a coming-out party?"

"What?"

"Like a Southern belle. A coming-out party. You can invite me and Jason and Matthew, or whoever you used to hang out with when you had friends. And wear a pretty gown. We'll bring presents."

"Why don't you just bring the presents and we can skip the gown?"

"Doesn't work that way."

"Well then, I don't want your presents. Besides, I know you're saving up to buy those blades."

"Already got 'em."

"What!?"

"I'm going to have to kiss that skating camp goodbye, but I made enough in my two weeks of working in frozen hell to buy these bad boys." Becky jumped off the bed and pulled a pair of shining new silver Rollerblades out of her book bag.

"I can't believe you didn't tell me sooner."

"I think your first homo kiss is bigger news than my Rollerblades. But now that we've covered that, check 'em out. Aren't they be-a-u-ti-ful? They've got bigger wheels, so I can basically break the speed of sound. And they give more ankle support, and the wheel alignment's better. I think I'm in love."

Alek examined the Rollerblades carefully, inhaling their new-store smell. "Where are the brakes, Becky?"

"Please. Brakes are for beginners. The harder tricks, like skating down rails, are impossible with brakes."

"Check you out."

"Well, I guess it's time for us to get rid of the things that are slowing us down," Becky said pointedly.

"Are we done talking about you?" Alek asked. "Because I need some advice."

"Don't let him get to second base until the third date. Guys think you're easy otherwise."

Alek smiled in spite of himself. "Where do you think this will look better?" he asked, taking a poster out of his closet and rolling it out for Becky to see.

"Who is that?"

"Andre Agassi."

"Isn't he, like, the best tennis player in the history of the game?"

"Was. He's retired now. This picture is from when he wasn't just the best player in the game, but also the hottest. My uncle gave it to me as a birthday present last year, and I've been wanting to put it up for months, and now I'm going to."

"Don't you think your folks will wonder why . . ."

". . . I'm putting up a poster of a famous half-Armenian athlete? 'I'm just honoring my heritage, Mom and Dad, like all good Armenian boys should.' "

"Look at you, already putting up posters of hot men. If being a gay guy doesn't work out for you, you can try being a straight teenage girl."

"Where should it go?"

"Put it over there. That way you can stare at it from your bed before you go to sleep every night."

Alek positioned the poster on the wall so that Becky could tell him if it was centered. After a few adjustments, they switched places so Alek could make sure he liked how it looked from the bed.

"I'm really glad you told me about this, Alek."

"Who else would I tell?" Alek replied simply.

Even though Alek felt like he *could* tell Becky anything, that didn't mean he *had* to tell her everything. For example, he had decided to omit Ethan's initial reaction to being kissed.

After recovering from the shock, Ethan had pulled away immediately. "I don't want a pity kiss from you, Alek."

"A what?"

"You felt bad for me because I was telling you about Remi, and that's why you kissed me."

The anger in Ethan's voice surprised Alek, but didn't deter

him. "Who's being crazy now, Ethan? If you don't want me to kiss you, I won't. But trust me, I'm not doing it out of pity."

Ethan considered this. "Yeah?"

"You heard me, *dude*," Alek responded, playfully punching him in the arm.

In the safety and privacy of Ethan's room, Alek felt freer and more confident than he ever had before. So when Ethan leaned in and kissed him back deeply, Alek responded in kind.

Alek looked at the absolute ordinariness of his own room. Transforming it so that it would be more him would be a challenge, but he felt ready to take it on.

"How's this?" Becky asked, adjusting the poster. "Is this good?"

"Move it a little to the right," Alek instructed Becky. "A little more—that's great!" He grabbed a pencil and started making marks on the wall.

"So, are you going to be, like, out now?" Becky asked.

Alek stopped in midmark. "What do you mean?"

"Well, are you and Ethan going to hold hands in school? Are you going to join the Gay-Straight Alliance in the fall? Are you going to become an expert on musical theater and fashion and wine?"

"I haven't thought about any of that. I mean, do you think people are going to treat me differently? Am I going to behave differently?"

"Alek, it's not like your personality's changed, or you just found out that you were adopted and that you're not really Armenian. You're still you. You're just a you that likes boys."

"I guess," Alek said. "But I hadn't thought about any of that other stuff."

"Well, I don't wanna stress you out, but you do need to think about it, because if you and Ethan even hold hands in school, it'll get back to your brother, and you know he'll tell your parents, and then—"

"Oh my God. My parents! They're gonna freak out!" Alek put the pencil down and sat on the floor. Until now, he'd been floating high on the thrill of having kissed Ethan. But these questions made him realize how much more he had to think about. "They've been talking about grandchildren for as long as I can remember. Producing grandchildren is one of the most fundamental of all Armenian responsibilities. It's more important than celebrating Remembrance Day or boycotting Turkish restaurants." Alek felt a sharp sensation in his hand. He looked down to see that he had snapped the pencil in half.

"Um, isn't it a little early to be thinking about kids? Don't you have to pick out kitchen curtains first?"

"I'm telling you, procreating is a sacred Armenian responsibility."

"So adopt."

"It's not that easy—passing along your DNA is part of what makes it so important."

"Alek, you have to calm down, okay?"

"That's easy for you to say. You're not the one about to be outed to your parents." Alek hadn't even thought about what he and Ethan would do in school. From the way Ethan spoke and carried himself, Alek knew that he wasn't scared of what other people thought. But Alek hadn't considered any of the consequences.

"Why don't you talk to Ethan about this? He's already gone

through it. This is where being the younger man is nice. I'm sure he'll know what to do. He always seems like he does."

"Thanks, Becky. That's a good idea. I'll try to put off my breakdown until then."

Alek hadn't thought about any of these things when he was with Ethan because Ethan's room felt like its own dimension, safe and far away from the rest of the world. Before he had left, Ethan played a Rufus track for Alek, insisting that he listen to the words.

"What a beautiful, sad song," Alek said.

"That's 'One Man Guy,'" Ethan responded. "It's my favorite Rufus. Do you get what he's saying in it?"

"I think so," Alek said. "It's about integrity, right? That people will understand that he's the kind of guy who'll stand up for what he believes in, and that he won't stand for the things he doesn't."

"That's right." Ethan beamed. "Rufus's dad recorded it years ago—he was a famous folk singer, so being a 'one man guy' to him was like a cowboy thing—alone on the range, doing the right thing. But do you understand why I wanted you to hear it?"

"You want to be a cowboy?"

"Funny, Alek, but you're not going to get off that easy. You see, when Rufus sings it, the song takes on a different meaning. When a gay guy sings, 'I'm a one man guy,' it means something more.

"After Remi, I used to think that I was going to be a one man guy the way Rufus's dad meant, alone in the world. But now I'm kissing you, and I want to be a one man guy the way Rufus means it. And I know this is new to you and you might not want to commit to anything right now, but that's the only way I can go on this ride. It's all or nothing with me."

Alek stared at Ethan, dumbfounded.

"I knew it!" Ethan said. "Remi told me never to get involved with someone just coming out. They're insecure, they don't know what they want, and they just use you as their homo experiment."

"How do you know I'm just coming out?" Alek asked.

"No disrespect," Ethan responded, "but you might as well have 'newbie' tattooed on your forehead."

"I just know that I like being here with you and can't imagine wanting anyone else. Is that good enough for now?"

"Good enough." Ethan pulled Alek onto his bed, where they held each other until they heard his father approaching the room again.

Alek smiled to himself as he remembered how quickly he had scurried off Ethan and to the opposite side of the room, just to be safe.

"What're you grinning about, Alek?" Becky asked, putting the poster down.

"It's a gay thing. You wouldn't understand," Alek answered.

13

THE SPOON ALEK WAS TAPPING AGAINST THE KITCHEN table later that day made a dull ringing sound. He wondered how many times he'd have to bang it against his head to knock himself unconscious. But if he did that, his parents might never leave.

"This is the phone number of the hotel where we'll be staying tonight," his mother explained again. "If you need us, just call and they'll connect you directly to our room. Of course, your father and I will also have our cell phones. Then after Wednesday, we'll be staying at the Marriott outside of . . . ."

This was the third time that his mom had gone over these instructions, and Alek could barely make the effort to pretend that he was paying attention. In the hallway that connected the front door to the kitchen, his father was making sure they'd packed everything they needed.

"Alek, are you listening to me? I want you to know how to

get in touch with us in case anything goes wrong," his mother said.

"You're only going to be gone for five days! Now, show me where you put the homing pigeons in case the flesh-eating zombies attack while you're gone and I need to ask you where you keep the Band-Aids."

"This isn't something to joke about, Alek. It's the first time we're leaving you alone and—"

"And everything's going to be fine, Mom," Alek reassured her.

Nik walked down the stairs, wearing a shirt and tie.

"Prom isn't until next spring," Alek cracked.

Instead of insulting him back, Nik looked flustered and turned to their mother. "Do you think it's too much, Mom?"

"Well, today we're going to be driving mostly. Maybe you could save that outfit for a nice dinner, honey."

Nik ran up the stairs.

"What's wrong with him? We don't dress that way unless we're going to church."

"I think, well . . ." his mother stumbled, clearing her throat.

"What is it, Mom?"

"I think Nik is worried about impressing Nanar's parents. They're so proper, you know. He's just worried he's not Armenian enough for them."

"If Nik doesn't cut it for them, they're going to need to get a mail-order groom delivered directly from Armenia," Alek said.

"Honey, I was thinking, if you want to do your summer shopping while we're gone, I'm leaving you this," his mother said, handing him an envelope. Alek opened it and found an American Express gift card.

"Oh my God!" Alek exclaimed. "Thanks, Mom," he said, embracing her spontaneously, surprising them both. "I swear I'll only buy clothes that are well-made and not from Turkey. And I'll keep all the receipts."

"I know. I trust you," his mother replied simply. "We're also leaving you this, just in case there's an emergency," she said, handing him an envelope full of cash.

Alek accepted it solemnly, thinking that he wished his family went on vacation without him more often.

"I had your father stock up on all the sundries, like soap and canned goods."

"I know. Between that and the twenty Tupperware containers full of food he left, if a nuclear war breaks out, I'll be able to support the entire neighborhood until the radiation levels drop."

Alek braced himself for the rebuke that was surely going to follow. Instead, she put her hand over his.

"We just want to make sure you have everything you need," she told him.

"I promise I'll be fine, Mom. Don't worry about it, okay?" Alek stroked her arm reassuringly.

"You're a good kid, Alek. I'm sorry I haven't—"

"Kadarine, can I talk to you for a moment?" Alek's father called from the corridor. "We have to figure out if we want to take I–95 all the way to I–80 or get on 287 and then switch over."

Alek's mom smiled at him warmly. "Don't worry about us too much when we're gone, okay? And remember: no more than one friend, no sleepovers, and call every morning and night." She stood up and left the kitchen, passing Nik on the way, who was now wearing skinny hipster jeans and a tapered, striped button-down. He was carrying a bundle of books, which he started putting into his suitcase.

"What're those, dear?" she asked him.

"I thought I'd bring along some summer reading I haven't gotten to yet." Nik held up one of the tomes. "This is a collection of plays by William Saroyan."

"Have you heard of him, Alek?" his mother asked hopefully.

"Let me guess. He's some Armenian guy who wrote plays?"

"He's the premier twentieth-century Armenian-American writer," Nik offered quickly. He held up another book. "And this is *The Forty Days of Musa Dagh*."

"That's the exposé about the Armenian Genocide by that German guy, right?" Alek offered. "Even I've heard of that one."

"He was Austrian, not German," Nik insisted.

"Whatev."

"Nik, what a great group of books you've assembled," his mother complimented him. "I'm sure Nanar's parents will be impressed." She kissed Nik on the forehead and went out to the car to help their dad pack up for the trip.

"You excited about your big trip?" Alek asked his brother.

"Yeah—we're going to start by going to North Point, and then by tomorrow we should make it up to Niagara Falls. You going to be okay by yourself all week?"

This sudden concern for Alek seemed to be afflicting everyone.

"I'll be fine. Just do me a favor, okay?"

Nik eyed Alek wearily. "Okay?"

"Don't spend the whole vacation reading those books. The whole point of going somewhere is to see that place."

"I know, Alek, but these books are on my summer reading list. I need to get through them."

Alek put his hand on his brother's shoulder. "Nik, there's a difference between *need* and *want*. Remember that, okay?"

Alek usually dreaded walking into the school cafeteria. But today, his heart was racing. This would be his first Ethan encounter since the kiss. A quick survey of the room revealed Ethan sitting with the Dropouts at their usual table.

The table was in the middle of the room, and the Dropouts easily made more noise than the rest of the cafeteria combined. Their dyed hair and metallic piercings made them pop out from the rest of the cafeteria like a highlighted sentence. Alek had to force himself to look away.

He started walking to the table where he usually sat. But after a few steps, he heard Ethan calling out to him.

"Wassup, Polly-O?"

"Hey, Ethan."

Just seeing him again sent shivers through Alek's body. Ethan's jeans hung low on his hips, and his hair fell on his face so that you could only see one of his blue eyes. He bounded over to Alek, hair flopping with every step.

"What are you doing?" he called out between bounds.

"Well, this is the cafeteria, so I figured I'd eat some lunch."

"Don't play with me, dude. I meant what are you doing walking back to that sad lonely table where you always sit by yourself? You sit with me from now on." Ethan put his hands on Alek's shoulders and guided him toward the table.

In all of the permutations that Alek had imagined for this interaction, he had never considered this one. He prayed that there wouldn't be a spot for him, but saw that Ethan had put his backpack on the seat next to his. Even at the D.O. table, no one would defile the holy high school code of saved seats.

"Good to meet you, Dropouts!" Alek blurted when they arrived at the table. Immediately, he wished he could take the words back. "Not that I think that, like, you guys are future dropouts or anything . . ." he fumbled, desperately trying to backpedal.

"We know what people call us," said a guy wearing a black leather jacket even though it was the middle of summer. "But we've come up with our own meanings."

"Like 'Dope Offensive,' " a guy with two eyebrow piercings shot back proudly, and the table cheered their approval.

"Or 'Destructive Obliteration,' " another guy on the other side of the table wearing a Bob Marley T-shirt said, earning another cheer.

"Or 'Devious Others,' " Alek added. But only silence followed his remark.

"I don't really think we're devious," one of the D.O.s said, a little defensively.

Alek didn't know which was worse—insulting Ethan's friends within a few seconds of sitting down at their table, or almost getting beat up by one of them a few weeks earlier.

"Anyway," Ethan cut in, "everyone, this is Alek. And that's Andy, Pedro, Anthony, Dustin, Chris, Mikey, Jack . . ." Alek didn't even try to remember all the names being fired at him. Whenever his parents had guests over, they had instructed Alek to shake hands upon acquaintance, making full eye contact.

Alek heard the words "Good to meet you, everyone" come out of his mouth. He knew he should've said something like, " 'Sup, dudes?" or just "Yo," or not even said anything and just given some super-cool hand gesture that would've somehow communicated that he didn't need words to earn their respect.

Alek was painfully aware of how out of place he was in this crowd. Wearing his khakis and a green short-sleeved Izod that his mom got him for his birthday, he looked down the table at a cornucopia of color, metal, and rough materials. Alek could tell that all of the Dropouts had been buying and wearing whatever they wanted to for years.

"How come he gets to sit here?" the guy with the doubly pierced eyebrow and shaggy hair complained from one end of the table.

Alek shifted in his seat, wondering why Ethan had chosen to subject him to this unique and cruel form of torture.

"What're you talking about, Pedro?" Ethan asked.

"Look, Ethan, when I was with Stephanie I wasn't allowed to bring her to our table. Do you know how pissed she was when I didn't sit with her during lunch? She said it was one of the major reasons that she dumped me."

"I think the fact that you didn't shower was another, Pedro," a guy with spiky bleached-blond hair responded. The entire table erupted with laughter.

"Good one, Josh," said an Asian-American D.O. next to him sporting a Mohawk.

"Don't be such a dick, Pedro. You know Stephanie couldn't sit with us because she's a chick," Ethan responded nonchalantly.

"So you're saying that because you're into dudes, the people you're with are allowed to sit with us?"

"I'm saying that only guys are allowed to sit at our table, so I'm allowed to invite Alek to sit with us."

"That blows."

"Think of it as a gay perk. Like not having to worry about pregnancy."

The table howled again, and Alek felt himself relax just a little bit. He had always lived outside of the Dropouts and observed them with awe and horror. You never saw a D.O. by himself: they always traveled the school in a pack, like wolves. But being at their table, he could see that they ate and fought and laughed like everyone else.

Alek leaned in to Ethan. "Does everyone here really know you're gay?"

"Yeah."

"Was it hard to come out to them?"

"In my head, it was really hard. None of them are gay, and I've known most of these guys since I was a kid. But one day during freshman year, at this very table, we were going around the table talking about which teacher we'd most like to bang. When it got to me, I said, 'Mr. Spack.'"

An image of the athletic history teacher with broad shoulders flashed into Alek's mind.

"At first they thought I was joking," Ethan continued. "But I wasn't. Josh"—Ethan pointed to the guy with spiky bleached-blond hair—"was like, 'So what does that mean? You're into dudes?' And I was like, 'You got a problem with that?' And Josh was like, 'No way—I'd definitely bang Mr. Spack over Ms. Schmidt,' and that was that."

"That easy?" Alek asked incredulously.

"Well, yes and no. Two seniors jumped me after school, but I sent them running."

"You beat up two upperclassmen when you were a freshman?"

"And got beat up by them," Ethan admitted sheepishly. "But after those two assholes graduated, everyone knew better than to give me shit."

One of the guys pounded his fist on the table. "No more whispering, girls."

"Shut it," Ethan hollered back.

Alek busied himself with unpacking his lunch.

"What you got there, dude?" the Asian-American D.O. sitting diagonally from Alek asked him.

"Yeah, it looks whack," Jack said. He got up from the far side of the table and walked over until he was directly across from Alek.

I can't believe I'm sitting across from the guy who almost beat me up just a few weeks ago, Alek thought to himself. He wondered if Jack remembered pinning him down on the other side of the tunnel.

Jack snatched the container out of Alek's hand. Alek felt Ethan about to react, but he jumped in first. He needed to show Ethan he could stand up for himself.

"They're *soudé* fruits," Alek said, while Jack continued to inspect the Tupperware that contained little purple bulbs soaking in brine. "Haven't you heard of them?"

"I haven't been to Bangladesh or wherever they come from."

"They're an Armenian delicacy, which makes sense because they only grow in Armenia. Something about the climate there, I guess. When they fall from the tree, they have to be harvested immediately; otherwise they become poisonous. But when you get them in time, they're delicious."

Jack climbed up and leaned over on the table to get a better look. The other guys stopped talking and looked over.

"I don't believe there's any such thing as a *soudé* fruit," Jack declared.

"Whatever, man." Alek threw the phrase away exactly the way he'd heard Ethan say it, letting the end drag off like he couldn't care less. "I guess that means you don't want to try one, which is too bad, 'cause it's the best damn thing you'll ever taste, but if you don't want it . . ."

Josh piped in from the end of the table. "I did a science report on them when I was in fifth grade. They're legit." Josh's hair was so blond it was almost white, and he spoke with a flat authority that dared to be contradicted. Alek didn't know if he'd ever sit at this table again, but after Ethan, Josh was his favorite D.O.

"I didn't say I didn't want to try it," Jack backpedaled.

"Nah, you're probably too scared." And to make his point, Alek grabbed the container out of Jack's hand, opened it, and popped one in his mouth. He chewed enthusiastically, letting the bliss of the experience show on his face. "Damn, that's good."

"Okay, man, hand one over," Jack said. When Alek pretended not to hear Jack, he barked, "I said give me one of those *soudé* fruits!"

"That's no way to talk to him, douchewad," Ethan barked back.

"It's cool, Ethan," Alek reassured him. He slid the container across the table, landing it next to Jack's hand. "You may want to try a little piece first, just to make sure you can handle it."

Jack looked at Alek defiantly, stuck his fingers into the Tupperware, snatched two of the dripping bulbs, and tossed them straight into his mouth. The entire table watched as he started chewing, slowly at first, and then more vigorously.

"Dude, you're right! They're awesome—tangy and—"

Alek put his hands on the table with concern. "Did you just say *tangy*?"

"Yeah."

"Oh my God!" Alek screamed, putting his hands on his face. "Spit it out, dude. Spit it out! The *soudé* fruit is supposed to be sweet. It's only tangy when they've been left on the ground too long. Then it's lethal!"

"Holy shit!" Jack screamed, spewing half-chewed purple chunks all over himself and the guys sitting close to him.

"Give him some water!" Alek yelled. Someone tossed Jack a water bottle from down the table, and he began gulping and spitting violently, trying to remove the remnants from his mouth.

"Call the nurse! Call 911!" Jack screamed between curses and eruptions.

"Dude, you're getting that shit everywhere!" one of the guys cried, wiping liquid off his face.

"Seriously," Alek agreed calmly. "You're totally overreacting."

"You were the one who said they were lethal!" Jack screamed.

"I was just kidding, man. God, can't you take a joke?"

"What?"

"You dumb-ass," Alek continued. "There's no such thing as a *soudé* fruit. These are just pickled eggplants. Baby eggplants, soaked in vinegar and brine until they shrink down to this size. They're harmless."

Everyone was silent as they processed what he'd said. This was the deciding moment, Alek realized: would they appreciate the joke he had played, or would they turn on him for humiliating one of their own ten minutes after he had been invited to sit down with them?

From down the table, Josh's blond hair bobbed up and down as he heaved with laughter. "You should've seen yourself, fool," he managed to get out between guffaws. "Spitting eggplant everywhere, freakin' out that you were gonna die. What a bitch. It was hilarious." Ethan started laughing a second later, and soon everyone joined in.

"You got served, dude," Dustin said, slapping Jack heartily on the back.

"He got you good," Pedro agreed.

Soon, even Jack joined in the laughter. The Dropouts' table was a mess: sodas had been spilled, lunch trays knocked over, sandwiches trampled on. But no one seemed to care.

"What does *soudé* mean, anyway?" Ethan asked.

"'It's a lie' in Armenian," Alek said, laughing now.

"Alek," Jack conceded through his own laughter, "you are one sick dude."

14

"LEMME GET THIS STRAIGHT. YOUR PARENTS ARE GONE for the week."

"Yup."

"You don't have anyone staying with you or looking after you?"

"Nope."

"And your mom left you some coin?"

"Yup."

"When's the party, dude?" Ethan exclaimed, leaping with joy.

Alek and Ethan were walking home after school that day, but for Alek, it felt more like floating than walking. After the *soudé* incident, Ethan's friends had warmed up to Alek. He knew he'd never be one of them, but he'd settle for not feeling like a total outsider when sitting at their table. Algebra was an exercise in tantalization, sitting so close to Ethan but not being able to talk to or touch him. Every now and then, Ethan would look over and catch Alek staring at him. Ethan would flash a trademark smile, then stare at Mr. Weedin intently, pretending to be engrossed in the lesson.

Alek and Ethan reached the entrance to the tunnel underneath the train station.

"What are you going to do now?" Alek asked.

"Well, usually I hang out and skate," Ethan said, dropping his board and hopping on top of it. "But I think you and I are going to have an impromptu New York City adventure today instead."

"Today? We can't go into the city today!"

"Why not?"

"For one thing, if my parents found out, they'd kill me!"

"And where are your parents right now?"

"Good point," Alek conceded. "But I still need to call them today. From the landline."

"No prob. Go home, call them, and be here in time to get on the 4:33. That'll still leave us plenty of time to spend some QT in the Big Apple."

Alek thought for a moment. Ethan's plan was solid. "I'll be there."

Ethan leaned in, gave Alek a kiss on his cheek, and walked away, his board slung over his shoulder.

Alek's cheek blazed. He stood, watching Ethan walk away. His cocky swagger had been the first thing to catch Alek's attention, as he strutted across the cafeteria or down a school corridor. The swagger said, *I'm my own man, and if you don't like it, I couldn't care less.* The elastic line of his underwear was peeking above his pants again. But this time, Alek didn't look away. Ethan suddenly turned around and caught Alek staring at him. He winked, blew him a kiss, then threw his board on the ground, jumped on top of it, and rolled away.

Alek went home and tried to figure out how this sudden jaunt to New York would affect his schedule. He had promised his parents that he'd mow the lawn that day, and he wanted to keep his word. He was also planning on writing a paper comparing *Romeo and Juliet* to *Love's Labour's Lost* for his English class, but since it wasn't due until Friday, he could put that off until tomorrow.

Alek was changing into his lawn-mowing clothes when the phone rang.

"Hello?"

"Hey, sexy," a deep voice breathed into the phone.

"Um, who is this?"

The husky voice continued, "I'm thinking about blading over there and showing you."

"Becky?"

"*C'est moi!*" she responded, dropping the act.

"What's going on?"

"We still on for tonight? I've got a great movie and some delicious microwavable kettle corn to celebrate your first night on your own. Well, second, I guess, since your folks left yesterday, but you know what I mean."

"Um, Becky, do you mind if we reschedule for tomorrow?"

"Well, you know what a busy social life I have. Hold on. Let me see. Do you want to tell me why you're canceling on me with such little notice while I flip through my calendar?"

"Ethan asked me to . . . Well, he thought it might be fun to go into the city tonight, what with my parents away and everything . . ." Alek stammered.

"And did you tell him that we had plans?"

"Honestly, I totally forgot until you just called."

A long pause followed.

"I know that I have every right to get pissed, but I'm going to take the higher road. That's how gracious I am. Like a princess. Like Audrey Hepburn in *Roman Holiday*. Alek, go and have fun tonight."

"Really? You're not mad?"

"Forget about it. Have a great time, reflect on what a great best friend you have, and we can watch *The Object of My Affection* tomorrow."

"You're the best, Becky."

Alek hung up the phone and changed into shorts and an old T-shirt.

The second hand of Alek's robot clock methodically clicked its way around the face while Alek spoke to his mom on the phone, one hour and one mowed lawn later.

"So everyone's having a good time?"

"Yes, Alek, thank you for asking. Today, we went on the *Maid of the Mist* cruise through Niagara Falls, and tomorrow we'll be visiting the Armenian community in Burlington, across the Canadian border, so the youth chapter can research their heritage projects. You know, you might think about joining next year."

"Sounds great, Mom."

Grass protruded from Alek's hair and stained his fingers. He knew that his parents could afford a motorized lawn mower, but his dad insisted on buying the manual kind because it would help his sons "build character."

"So, everything's good?"

"Well, almost everything."

"What is it, Mom?" Alek walked over to the shower and turned the water on so he could jump in the second he got off the phone.

"It's just, traveling with the Hovanians can be so trying. Nothing is ever good enough for them. Why, just today, Mrs. Hovanian insisted on going into the kitchen of the Armenian restaurant where we had lunch to show them how to make real kibbi."

"Well, you know *these Armenians . . .*" he joked, and was rewarded by the sound of his mother's laughter.

"*These Armenians* indeed," she agreed.

"Well, if there's nothing else . . ." Alek said.

"Are you in a rush, darling?"

Alek eyed the clock nervously. It was almost four o'clock, so he only had a few minutes to get off the phone if he wanted to get to the station on time.

"Of course not, Mom," Alek covered. Somehow, Alek's mom could always tell when something else was going on. It's the reason he asked his dad, and not her, to sign the math test when he needed to forge the excused-absence note for the first New York trip, which he ended up having to do again when he visited Becky at Dairy Queen after his fight with Ethan. Sometimes, he wondered if all Armenian mothers possessed telepathic abilities, or just his own.

"So how was school?"

"It was *fine*, Mom."

"You know, Ms. Schmidt told us that you're doing very well. If you continue like this, you'll have no problem placing on Honor Track come fall."

"Yup. Do you like your hotel?"

"Well, I asked for a different room, because the first one smelled of chemicals. I think they must've just shampooed the carpeting, and as grateful as I am for their cleanliness, you know how sensitive my olfactory is. The second room is better, but the view isn't as good . . ." His mind wandered as his mom rattled off about the intricate pros and cons of hotel rooms.

Staring at the shorts he had laid on his bed, Alek wished that he had something cooler to wear for this New York adventure. But he had looked at every pair of pants and shorts he owned, and they all felt equally dorky to him.

". . . I just hope the food at the restaurant is okay."

"I'm sure it'll be fine."

"Have you done your summer clothes shopping yet?"

"I was thinking about asking the Boyces to drive me and Becky to the mall this week."

"That's a great idea. Just make sure that what you buy fits you well."

"Thanks, Mom."

"And use the gift card. You know how much we usually spend, right?"

Alek had anticipated this. "I think you left enough cash for the clothes—why don't I just use that? And I'll save the card for if there's an emergency. Do you mind?" he asked.

"Either way, honey. I have to get ready for dinner. Your father and Nik and Nanar send their love."

"Holla back for me."

"Excuse me?"

"I mean, say hi to them from me, too." Alek hung up the phone, threw his clothes into the hamper, and jumped in the shower.

"Hurry hurry hurry!" Ethan screamed from the platform. By the time Alek reached the train station, he was panting from having run the whole way. Alek bolted up the stairs a second before the train stopped and the doors opened. He put his hands in his pockets, feeling the objects that he had grabbed as he ripped out of his house: keys, the envelope full of cash, and the Metropolitan Museum sticker for good luck.

"You were freakin' me out, dude. What took so long?"

"Mom . . . phone . . . longer . . ." Alek managed to sputter between breaths.

"We gotta get moving, man. You remember the drill."

"Yessir!"

Alek snuck into the bathroom, leaving the door open, as Ethan opened his book bag and took out a black Sharpie and piece of white construction paper.

Alek felt the train dip into a tunnel. From the first trip, he remembered they'd pull into Penn Station in a few minutes.

"So what're we doing tonight?"

"We're gonna kick it downtown style today."

Alek didn't really know what Ethan meant, but he had learned to trust that things would be explained to him on a need-to-know basis.

"I have a request," Alek stated.

"You do, do you?" Ethan cocked one eyebrow inquisitively.

"I want you to take me shopping."

"I think it's a little early for us to be picking out curtains. We're not lesbians, after all."

"That's not what I mean, Eth. I want clothes like yours. Cool clothes."

"Just because we're together doesn't mean you have to dress like me, Alek. I like the way you dress. It's dorky-chic."

"I think it's just dorky-dorky. I'm not saying I want to dress like you, but . . ." Alek trailed off. His parents had always criticized *these Americans* who bought clothes every month to reflect the latest fashion, and Alek certainly didn't want to be one of those people. But he was tired of dressing in a way that didn't feel like himself. Even if it meant having to go to school in his underwear, Alek vowed to never wear khakis again.

"Well, you're in luck, dude," Ethan said. "I do all of my shopping downtown, so it'll be easy enough to hit a store or two. We'll see what you like. You know, though, it's going to take some coin."

"I'm on it." Alek produced the cash from his pocket and showed it to Ethan.

"Whoa, dude. You can't go around flashing green like that once we're in the city."

Sheepishly, Alek stuffed the envelope back into his pocket.

"So, MetroCard two-for-one special?"

"Not today. The weather's so great, and we're not in a rush. We're going to walk our way through Manhattan. It's the best way to get to know this city."

"Lead, and I will follow."

"I know you will." Ethan leaned in and kissed Alek gently on the lips. The train came to a halt. "Let's go."

15

"SO WHAT ARE WE GOING TO DO FIRST?"

"We're gonna get you a new look. What're you thinking?"

"I just don't want to wear these stupid khaki shorts anymore."

"You have to figure out what you want to look like. People don't dress cool by accident. It's gotta be planned, even if it looks like it's not. I think you need to look at a few options. Luckily, I know just the place."

The summer breeze offset the heat, and the humidity was blessedly low. Alek and Ethan walked through a group of street acrobats leaping over one another in synchronized daredevilry to hip-hop music in front of a huge rotating, glowing cube sculpture that looked like an artifact from the future.

"Downtown feels totally different from Museum Mile and Central Park," Alek observed.

"That's what rocks about New York. It's like a thousand different cities stuck together on one little island."

"Everything uptown was so clean and organized. But down here, it's more . . ."

"Caj?" Ethan offered.

"Caj?"

"You know. Casual. And artsy. Downtown is artsy," Ethan said. "That's a good way to think about your new look. Before, you were clean and organized, like uptown. But now, you're going to discover the downtown, artsy Alek."

"The artsy Alek," Alek repeated to himself.

Alek and Ethan walked into a small park surrounded by streets and stores. Alek could make out UNION SQUARE NORTH on a nearby street sign.

"You gotta check this out!" Ethan grabbed Alek's hand and practically ran to the other side of the square, where a bunch of kids were skateboarding up and down rails, ramps, and stairs.

"It looks just like what you guys have back home," Alek said.

"This was our inspiration. It doesn't matter what time of the day it is, a bunch of kids are always at it out here. And check them out!

"Awesome moves, dude," Ethan called out to a skateboarder who jumped onto the rail with his board, slid down, flipped it around in midair, and landed with ease. The skater responded by punching his chest twice and throwing Ethan a peace sign.

After watching the skateboarders for a few more minutes, Alek and Ethan continued walking south. A few blocks later, they made a left on Astor Place.

"Okay. I know that you didn't ask for it, but if we're gonna make you over, we've gotta start with the hair."

"Ethan, you might think of yourself as some kind of miracle

worker, but you haven't met my Armenian 'Fro. This will be my hair until I die."

"You don't know my man Marco. The guy's a genius."

Ethan walked down a staircase under a barber's sign in which the words "ASTOR HAIR" were formed with white lightbulbs against a black background. Alek quickly followed. He emerged into a basement labyrinth of mirrors and barber chairs, so dark that Alek didn't know how the barbers could see anyone's hair, let alone cut it. This place bore no resemblance to the brightly lit, elevator-music hair salons at the mall, where Alek's mom had been taking him his whole life.

Everything in this room was in motion—barbers furiously snipping, assistants anxiously sweeping, and electric razors boldly buzzing. The customers were mostly grown-up men, but Alek could see kids who looked younger than him and some senior citizens navigating the room with canes and walkers. Even the clients sitting in the chairs had a glow of energy around them, animatedly discussing local politics or sports with one another across cutting stations. Ethan didn't pause to take in the pandemonium. He beelined to a barber in the back of the room.

"Ethan, *mio caro*, great to-ah see you!" a pudgy middle-aged man with a few days' worth of stubble, a thick bushy mustache, and an even thicker accent called to him.

"Marco, this is my friend Alek. Save him!" Ethan called. Marco had warm brown eyes, and his fat fingers, squeezed into the scissor handles, looked like sausages about to pop out of their casings.

Marco pulled Ethan and Alek aside. "I-ah finish with my-ah current client in five-ah minutes. There's a wait list, but any friend-ah Ethan's a friend-ah mine." Marco ran his sausage fingers through Alek's hair. "Greek?"

"Armenian."

"That-ah would've been-ah my-ah next guess. Only the Greeks and the Armenians have-ah hair this-ah crazy. We-ah see what we can do, eh? You should be-ah wearing your-ah hair, not the other way around, yes?"

Half an hour later, Alek emerged from the basement sporting his new short, tousled hair. In spite of the detailed instructions he'd received, Alek had no idea if he'd ever be able to re-create that perfectly messy look that Marco could achieve in fifteen seconds by squirting some product in his hands and running them over Alek's head.

"Check out my boy!" Ethan said admiringly when Alek stepped out of the barber shop. Alek saw his reflection in a glass storefront. The cut looked even more drastic in the light of day than it had in Marco's dark mirror downstairs. He'd never realized how his old hair had drawn focus away from his eyes, nose, and ears. With this new shorter do, his features jumped into the foreground.

"I feel exposed."

"Scary, isn't it, to have nothing to hide behind?" Ethan asked.

"Yes," Alek agreed. "But also freeing."

"Dude, it looks freakin' hot." Ethan took a deep breath and screamed out, "My boy looks hot!"

"Shh!" Alek looked around to see if anyone had responded to Ethan's outburst.

But Ethan had already moved on. "Now we need to get this hottie some hot clothes," he continued. "Let's go."

Ethan and Alek walked for another fifteen minutes until they stood outside of a brick building with the words HOUSING WORKS stenciled on the windows and door. "Follow me," Ethan said, entering the store without breaking his pace. Alek did.

"Ethan!" a young African-American woman called from behind the register. "You haven't been here in ages—it's good to see you, babe!"

"Clarice! What up, girl?" Ethan said, leaning over and giving her a hug. "This is Alek. Alek, this is Clarice. She's finishing up at FIT—Fashion Institute of Technology—so you know she's legit." Then he turned back to Clarice. "I'm thinking preppy/artsy/nerdy chic. Can you help us?"

"Follow me," she said. When Clarice walked out from behind the counter, Alek could appreciate her full ensemble. She wore tight purple pants and a sleeveless black shirt with sequins that shimmered whenever she moved. Ethan and Alek followed Clarice as she navigated through the clothes racks.

"This is a used-clothes store!" Alek exclaimed.

"How do you think I remain so fashionable on a budget?" Ethan asked. "But it's not *just* a used-clothes store."

"We donate our profits to homeless people with HIV or AIDS," Clarice told Alek as she guided them through the racks of clothing. "So you get to look tight and support a good cause."

"They've also got a bookstore downtown," Ethan said. "Not that I've spent much time there."

"Now let's see." Clarice appraised Alek like a scientist trying to puzzle the results of an experiment. "No pale earth tones or yellows—I like you in rich primaries, and maybe a luscious brown to bring out those eyes. That sound right to you, Ethan?"

"Spot-on as always, Clarice."

"What about this?" she asked, pulling out a faded green T-shirt.

"That's the Green Lantern insignia!" Alek exclaimed with joy, admiring the white circle graphic on the chest of the shirt.

"What?" Ethan said.

" 'In brightest day, in blackest night, no evil shall escape my sight.' That's the Green Lantern motto!"

"Whatever," Ethan said. "I just think it looks fierce. You hold, Clarice and I grab," he said, throwing Alek the shirt.

Soon Alek was buried in a pile of clothes. He immediately vetoed some of the stuff as too weird, like a pair of bright red flare pants and a neon purple tank top. But Ethan didn't mind. "We're just figuring out what you like."

When Alek thought he'd crumble under the weight of the pile of clothes he was holding, Ethan said, "Take these and try them on. I'll be there in a sec."

Alek found the dressing room in the back corner of the store and waited in line until it was available.

Sliding the curtain closed behind him, Alek slipped his shoes and khaki shorts off and tried on the first pair of pants, slim-fitting dark blue trousers with a button fly and stitching on the sides in neon-orange accents.

"Alek, get out here and model for me!" Ethan screamed from outside. Shyly, Alek slid the curtain open and walked out.

" 'The rain in Spain stays mainly in the plain,' " Alek recited in a British accent.

"Excuse me?" Ethan appraised the pants' fit on Alek from all angles.

"That's what Eliza Doolittle is taught to say correctly when she's finally transformed in *My Fair Lady*."

"Whatever, man. Those look gorgeous. Try them with . . ." Ethan ran into the dressing room and pulled out a tight black V-neck T-shirt.

Alek changed shirts and walked out in the full ensemble. Ethan whistled in approval. "This is what you're going to be wearing when you walk out of here. Go in there and show me the rest of it."

Ethan's enthusiasm drew everyone in. When Alek walked out a few moments later, this time wearing the Green Lantern T-shirt with low-riding gray boot-cut jeans, the other customers waiting in the dressing room line clapped. Ethan made him model the clothes up and down the aisle, much to the impromptu audience's pleasure.

"You've got to get some kick-ass shoes for that getup," a trim, well-dressed young man holding a briefcase suggested.

"Those two make an adorable couple," a middle-aged woman in a beige straw hat whispered to her friend.

Back in the dressing room, Alek pulled the shirt off and was deciding what to try next when he heard Ethan from the other side of the curtain.

"I picked these up for you. I want to see if you look better in the black or silver frames. I think we're ready to move into accessories." Alek caught a glimpse of himself in the mirror, shirtless, before Ethan barged in, holding two pairs of sunglasses and a few chains of wood beads.

"Oh, uh, I didn't realize . . . Sorry, I assumed you were dressed," Ethan sputtered when he saw Alek half-naked. But he didn't make any movement to leave.

"I was just trying to figure out what to try next," Alek responded, turning around so his back was to Ethan.

"How about this one?" Ethan held up an almost transparent white button-down covered with a floral Southwestern design over the shoulders and back.

"Great, you want to leave it?" Alek asked.

"I'd rather you turned around so I could see you put it on."

Alek paused for a second before he slowly turned around. He could see Ethan look him up and down. Although he should've been uncomfortable, Alek secretly felt thrilled to be seminaked in front of Ethan. And having so many people close by made it even more exciting.

"I didn't realize you had such sexy tris." Ethan spoke slowly, taking his time with each word.

"Tris?"

"Triceps, duh."

"I told you I played tennis for years."

Ethan put a finger on Alek's elbow and traced his triceps up to his shoulder. Alek felt every hair on his body go rigid in response. Ethan's finger lingered on Alek's shoulder for a while, and then slowly, it wound its way forward, tracing down his pecs.

"And I didn't realize how well you tan. Do all Armenians tan this well?"

"Well, lots of Armenians are really pale, like my mom. That's where my brother gets it from. But I look more like my dad. He's so dark, he's sometimes mistaken for Turkish."

"Thank God for Dad's dark Armenian genes."

Ethan's finger slid up under Alek's chin, and then he pushed him against the dressing room wall. Ethan leaned his body against Alek's and kissed him.

"Not here!" Alek protested weakly after a few seconds.

"I don't care where we make out." Ethan smiled slyly but pulled away. His body language, however, made it clear that he would've happily continued kissing. And maybe more. "But it's cool. Let me see you in that button-down."

Standing in the checkout line a few minutes later, Alek couldn't believe that the two pairs of pants, three pairs of shorts, and four shirts he was holding, not to mention the blue pants and black V-neck outfit that Ethan chose for him, with the silver sunglasses and a string of wooden beads around his neck, totaled less than half the money his mother usually spent on his summer clothes.

"And how about this, to pull it all together?" Ethan asked, holding up a beat-up brown leather backpack.

Alek dropped his clothes on the floor and held the backpack in a loving embrace.

"Goodbye, JanSport," he said, nuzzling the bag with his nose and inhaling its old leather smell.

"I'll take that as a yes?" Ethan asked, picking up Alek's clothes from the floor.

A few minutes later, they stood outside the Housing Works store, Alek proudly wearing his new clothes, the rest of them folded into the leather backpack strapped on his back.

"You remember the five bucks we didn't spend last trip because you were being all salty?"

"I wasn't salty, whatever that means! I thought you were being homophobic . . ."

". . . when I was just being homosexual," Ethan quipped. "You hungry?"

With all of the day's activities, Alek didn't realize he hadn't eaten since the *soudé* incident.

"Starved!"

"That's what the remaining five bucks go to. Food. Even in New York City, you can find good cheap food."

Ethan turned and Alek followed. *What must it be like,* Alek wondered, *to actually know your way around this city?*

"We're going to grab a bite, and then we're going to hit the High Line."

"What's the High Line?"

"You'll have to see it to believe" was all Ethan would say.

Alek and Ethan passed countless restaurants, stands, and food carts as they traveled through the city. "Can't we just grab something at one of these?" Alek asked.

"No," Ethan responded quickly. "This place is a little bit out of our way, but if you want the best, you have to be willing to travel for it. Especially if you want the best on a budget."

They passed a basketball court, and Ethan took a sharp left. "We're in the West Village. It used to be the bohemian/gay neighborhood, but then gentrification happened, and now only rich people live here. And NYU students. Here we are."

Ethan stopped in front of a small, white-and-brown-striped awning attached to a sign that read MAMOUN'S FALAFEL.

"Falafel!" Alek exclaimed.

"Don't tell me falafel is Armenian, too?"

"It's not—it's Middle Eastern. But my mom grew up next door to an Egyptian family, and their moms traded recipes all the time. Falafel is to me what hot dogs were to most kids."

Ethan stepped up to place their order, but Alek interceded. "I got this," he said. "We'll take two falafel sandwiches, and give me the real pitas—not that thick stuff *these Americans* like." The guy behind the counter nodded at Alek approvingly. He grabbed some thin pitas from beneath the counter, opened them up, then used a pair of tongs to pick up some falafel balls from the fry basket.

"How long has that falafel been sitting there?" Alek asked the guy, who looked down sheepishly instead of answering. "That's what I thought," Alek continued. "You mind whipping us up a new batch, please?" The guy scooped some mashed chickpeas into balls and dropped them into the boiling oil.

"You really know your way around a falafel stand," Ethan commented, impressed.

"You have no idea how proud my parents would be of me right now," Alek replied. When the falafel was ready, Alek pointed to the toppings. "You can go light on the salad, and then give us some of those cucumbers in brine and—"

"Some *soudé* fruits!" Ethan exclaimed with joy.

"And some pickled eggplant would be great. And we'll take the tahini and the hot sauce, please. *Sahtein*," Alek said as the man handed him the falafel sandwiches.

"What does *sahtein* mean?" Ethan asked.

"It's like *bon appétit* in Arabic," Alek responded.

"Will those be together?" the man asked, ringing them up.

"Yes, please," Alek jumped in before Ethan had a chance to respond. He handed the cashier a ten-dollar bill from the envelope and slipped another dollar into the tip jar.

"Alek, you don't have to pay for me."

"I know I don't. But this is a date, right?"

"Preach."

"Assuming that means 'yes,' it would be my pleasure."

"Check me out. My boyfriend bought me a falafel sandwich," Ethan boasted to the Goth girls behind them.

"You two are so cute. And you're so lucky. Gay is so 'in' right now. I'm totally thinking about going lesbo," the taller one responded.

Alek would've laughed or at least acknowledged the girl's comment, but he was still absorbing Ethan's use of the word *boyfriend*. They ate while they walked, Ethan practically dragging Alek along.

"My mom says it's not healthy to walk and eat," Alek protested.

"Your mom doesn't have to get to the High Line before it closes."

They walked up and then over, and Ethan guided Alek up a circular outdoor staircase. A walking garden, running parallel to the river and suspended in the middle of the city, welcomed them.

"This is so cool!" Alek cried.

"I know, right?" Ethan nodded. "This used to be a train track that would deliver milk, meat, produce, and raw and manufactured goods into the city. Then it was closed down for, like, forever, and people wanted to tear it down, but someone had the idea to turn it into a park. Come on!"

"It's like the opposite of Central Park," Alek observed as they strolled.

"How do you mean?"

"Well, in Central Park, you forget you're in a city. Here, the city and nature meld into this incredible hybrid thing. The High Line couldn't exist anywhere else."

"No, it couldn't," Ethan agreed. "I just love the way the city looks from this second-floor perspective." He pointed west. "That's where the Ramblers, the city's gay soccer team, play every Monday night. And down there is the Hotel Chelsea, which used to be *the* place to be. And look, this is one of my favorite parts," he said when they reached 26th Street. They sat suspended over the street, watching it stretch into what looked like infinity. "You never get to see a street or avenue from this angle. Isn't it amazing?" Ethan asked.

Alek nodded yes, watching the street stretch into the horizon.

They passed couples holding hands and more food carts. When they reached a Mexican paleta stand, Ethan proudly produced his own wallet. "If you can buy me falafel, then I can buy you dessert," he said, and purchased one strawberry and one mango chili frozen fruit bar. "You wanna go splitsies?" Ethan asked.

"On a popsicle?" Alek exclaimed.

"Scared of catching my germs?"

They continued walking as they ate their dessert, admiring the floating park's architecture and how it seamlessly melded into the foliage and greenery. "Come on, come on," Ethan hurried Alek along. "We don't have much time left."

"Time left for what?"

"Just hurry up!" Ethan said, practically dragging him down another circular staircase. Alek followed Ethan across a highway onto a small grass-lined pier.

"We're all the way west in Manhattan." Ethan pointed to the

road that ran parallel to the water. "This is the West Side Highway."

"I keep on forgetting that Manhattan is an island," Alek admitted.

He looked up and saw the sun setting behind the Jersey sky-
line. Alek had grown up in New Jersey and knew that it had the
reputation of being the nation's armpit. And usually Alek felt
like the reputation was well-earned. But now, a few stray rays of
sun shot up, piercing the darkening sky with shafts of purple,
red, and orange. The reflection shimmered on the water deli-
cately, as though any disturbance would cause the image to disappear. Even New Jersey, Alek thought, looked beautiful through
the lens of New York. Alek and Ethan stood, admiring.

"You called me your boyfriend back there at the falafel place,"
Alek said softly, still looking straight ahead.

"At Mamoun's?"

"Yeah. You told those girls that your boyfriend bought you
some food."

"So?"

Alek paused, wondering if he could build up his courage to
ask the terrifying question.

"Why me, Ethan? You're so—well—you could have anyone
in the school that you wanted. Why did you choose me?"

"I have a soft place in my heart for the Armenian people. The
whole genocide thing . . ." The breeze was gently billowing wisps
of Ethan's hair. Alek thought he could be content to spend the
rest of his life like this, with the sun and the water and the wind
and Ethan. But that didn't mean he was going to let him evade
the question.

"I'm being serious, Ethan," Alek insisted softly. He put his hand on Ethan's, interlocking their fingers on the rail.

Ethan took a long, considered pause before he started speaking. "I think, when you're our age, it's really easy to do the easy thing. I mean, what adults don't understand, or maybe they've just forgotten, is that most of the time we mess up, we know we're doing something stupid, but we choose to do it anyway because it's easier. But you're different. You're not scared to do the right thing, even when it's harder. Like telling Mr. Weedin when he had copied that problem wrong. Or calling me out when you thought I was being homophobic. And I respect that, Alek. You've got character. That's something I want in a guy I'm going to be with. It means he's going to treat me well, and that he deserves to be treated well himself."

Alek leaned his head on Ethan's shoulder and continued watching the last few remnants of the sun disappear.

"One more thing," Ethan said after a long pause. "And this was true before today, but now it's indi-freakin'-sputable." He put his arm around Alek's shoulder and whispered into his ear. "You're sexy, boyfriend."

16

ALEK HAD LAID OUT HIS CLOTHES THE NIGHT BEFORE, making a covenant with himself to wear them. Even so, he had to make himself ignore the comforting invisibility of the old mall fare in his closet. When he walked on the High Line yesterday, his new clothes made perfect sense. But as he lay on his bed in New Jersey, they felt as out of place as fireworks at a funeral.

Alek didn't know if it was a good sign that Ms. Imbrie, his English teacher, didn't recognize him when he walked in that morning, wearing tight jeans and a short-sleeved red plaid button-down shirt and sporting his new tousled hair. And although he certainly wasn't dressed like a D.O., he felt much more comfortable at their table wearing his new threads. Josh, with the bleached spiky hair, even said, "Um, dude, I'm straight and I'd totally do you." To which Ethan quickly responded, "Josh, you're straight?" and the table howled.

. . .

"Do you want something to drink?" Alek asked Ethan later that day after school as they walked into his living room.

"Some water would be great."

"Plain or fizzy?"

"Fizzy's good."

"Chilled or room temperature?"

"You guys keep fizzy water chilled *and* at room temperature?"

"A good host is prepared for all possibilities," Alek responded, quoting his mom.

Ethan had stretched out on the sofa by the time Alek returned with the room-temperature fizzy water. He set it down on a coaster in front of Ethan and sat down on the chair opposite him.

"Why are you sitting so far away, boyfriend? I don't bite," Ethan purred. Lying on his stomach, his back arched into the sunlight streaming in from the living room window, Ethan looked positively feline.

Alek walked over slowly and sat down on the other side of the sofa. This was really the first time that the two of them had been together alone in a private place since their first kiss. The possibilities terrified Alek and thrilled him.

As if reading his mind, Ethan said, "You're still too far away."

Alek scootched over so that his knees were right next to Ethan's reclined head. Ethan put his head on Alek's lap, arched up, and kissed him firmly on the lips.

When Alek had learned about the Trojan War and Helen of Troy as the face that launched a thousand ships, he found the whole story totally unbelievable. The idea that a single person could attract, inspire, or arouse hundreds of men to risk their lives and livelihood felt like the kind of mythological hyperbole that never really happened in the real world. But while kissing Ethan, Alek understood why all those Ancient Greek warriors got on those ships and sailed to the other side of their world.

Much of what Ethan had already taught Alek had been by description; how the streets of Manhattan were organized, or the deeper meaning of a Rufus Wainwright song. But this was teaching by example, and Alek was an eager student. Alek learned when to lean in and when to pull back, when to nibble and when to breathe.

Ethan began gently running his fingers through Alek's hair. The increase in pressure was so subtle that Alek didn't notice it at first, but soon, the motion evolved into something stronger. Eventually, Ethan grabbed a fistful of Alek's hair by the roots. Alek surprised himself by interrupting one of their kisses with a deep, guttural moan. Ethan grabbed again, and Alek moaned even louder.

"You like that, do ya, boyfriend?" Ethan smiled deviously at Alek.

"Uh-huh," Alek responded. Even a few days ago, he might've blushed, but now he didn't.

Ethan's hands worked their way down to the top of Alek's shirt. Alek inhaled sharply, realizing that he'd lost all track of time, and had no idea if he and Ethan had been making out for a few minutes or for hours.

Being with Ethan like this also terrified Alek. The first time they'd kissed, in Ethan's room, enough factors had conspired to limit the experience: they knew Mr. Novick would be coming home eventually, and also, Alek had never kissed a boy before. But today, stretched out in his family living room without the threat of interruption, Alek had no idea how to slow things down, or how much he'd be comfortable with. And part of him was scared that he wouldn't *want* to do either of those things, that he'd lose himself in his curiosity and hunger.

One by one, Ethan's hands unbuttoned their way down Alek's red plaid short-sleeved shirt. When they got to the bottom, they lingered on the top button of his new jeans. Alek jerked away from Ethan.

"I'm just kidding with you, dude." Ethan laughed. "We're not going to be ready for that for a while. At least another few days."

"What?" Alek said, terrified and excited.

"Man, I'm just playing with you. Where'd your sense of humor go? Just shut up and kiss me. You're getting good at it."

Ethan whipped off his own T-shirt and put his hands on Alek's head, drawing him in again. The sound of the doorbell interrupted their embrace.

"Just leave it, dude," Ethan begged. "Whoever it is will go away."

"What if my parents asked the Eisingers to check on me?"

"Who cares, man?"

"I care—now put your shirt on," Alek insisted.

"Are you kidding me?"

"Do I sound like I'm kidding?" Alek asked, throwing Ethan's shirt at him.

"I'm not embarrassed about being gay, you know."

"Neither am I, but this isn't how I plan on coming out to my parents, okay? Now dress!" Alek commanded as he went to his front door.

"I brought the movie, a bag of Cracker Jack, and, of course, Diet Dr Pepper," he heard Becky say before the door was open all the way. "I'm assuming your folks left enough to feed a small army, right? Because if not . . ." Becky trailed off when she saw Alek. "Alek? Is everything all right? What happened to your hair?"

"Hey, Becky—is it six already? I totally forgot we had plans."

"I can tell," Becky said, eyeing him and his half-open shirt up and down.

"Hello, lady," Ethan called from the living room.

Becky looked from Alek to Ethan, back to Alek. "You must be Ethan."

"And you must be?"

"I'm Becky. I'm assuming Alek has mentioned his best friend to you?"

"The inline skater!"

"Bingo."

"Killer wheels you got. Are those Kinetics?"

"Close—Activas."

Alek couldn't believe it. Even in this situation, Ethan could keep his cool.

"Some of my friends and I skate on the other side of the tunnel," Ethan continued. "We're mostly boarders, but we've got some skaters, too. I'd invite you to come and hit it sometime, but we have a strict no-girls rule."

"Ethan, if that's a challenge, consider me game. I'm sure I could teach you and the D.O.s a thing or two."

Alek cleared his throat not so subtly. "Becky, Ethan and I were sorta . . ."

"Yeah, I have a pretty clear sense of what you two were sorta doing. But you already blew me off once and you're not going to do it again. Ethan, you're more than welcome to join us if you'd like. And I think it's a good idea if the three of us start spending some time together anyway. You might be Alek's boyfriend, but I'm his best friend, I've known him longer, I know him better, and I'm not going anywhere, so you better get used to me."

Becky marched into the adjoining den. "I'm just going to set everything up," she called from the TV room. "Hurry up! I've been dying to watch this one. Again. It's got Jennifer Aniston and Paul Rudd in it. *The Object of My Affection* isn't an old movie, but it's so good, it may as well be. Jennifer Aniston gets knocked up by her boyfriend, but she dumps him and decides to bring the baby up with Paul Rudd, her gay best friend, who she's fallen in love with. Ring any bells?"

Alek stood dumbfounded.

"That lady's really got some spunk, don't she?" Ethan asked Alek. "Remind me never to piss her off."

"Are you guys coming?" Becky called from the den. "The credits are playing!"

Two hours later, the end credits rolled on the screen. "Great flick," Ethan said. He and Becky sat on the sofa, while Alek sprawled out on the floor. "It's nice to see some gay characters who are just, like, you know, normal. When did it come out?"

"1998," Becky said, reading the cover.

"So ahead of its time."

"I'm glad you liked it, Ethan. I would've told Alek to break up with you if you didn't." Even between her predictable sobs, Becky could keep her game up. "I like how there's so much going on in that movie, like a woman having a baby by herself, and the importance of promises that friends make each other." Becky turned to Alek. She blew her nose into a tissue and wiped her eyes. "You know what I mean?"

"I do now," Alek said, meaning it.

"What did you think of the movie, boyfriend?" Ethan asked Alek, scooting down on the floor to be next to him.

"Yeah, Alek. You're being suspiciously quiet."

Alek considered a moment before responding. "I was just thinking—I wonder how long it takes an idea to change."

"What do you mean?" Becky had exhausted the tissue and was now using the back of her sleeve to wipe her nose.

"We have this idea of family, right, that's been around for the last few thousand years. And at the end of this movie, we see a different idea of family."

"Or lots of different ideas of family," Ethan said.

"Exactly—gay, straight, older, interracial—and I was just wondering, how long will it be before we have more than one idea of family in our heads."

"How many kids our age do you know who come from 'normal families' anyway? I only see my mom a few times a year. Most of my friends' folks are divorced or not speaking. I think it's about time that our idea of family caught up with reality," Ethan said.

"Well, most of the time, reality doesn't make any sense, and I think that's one of the reasons the movie is so good," Becky said. She picked up a discarded bag of pretzels and started munching on them. "Like when Jennifer Aniston and Paul Rudd started to make out. They were best friends, she knew he was gay, and if his ex-boyfriend hadn't called just that minute, who knows how far they would've gone."

"I've never made out with a girl," Ethan said.

"Really?" Alęk said. It would've never occurred to him that he might be more experienced than Ethan in certain ways.

"Nope. I mean, who knows—I might go to college and experiment with members of the opposite sex, but so far, the impulse hasn't occurred to me."

"Well, I think about making out with girls sometimes," Becky said, popping the DVD out of the player.

"No way," Alek said.

"Sure." Becky shrugged. "But then again, I think women's sexuality is much more fluid."

"Than what?" Ethan asked.

"Than men's," Becky said.

Alek leaned forward. "Oh yeah? And what do you know about male sexuality?"

"Well, there's this guy I used to make out with—" Becky started.

"You never told me this!"

"Must have slipped my mind," Becky continued with studied nonchalance. "That guy Brock who lives on my grandma's street in Maine."

"Him!? I can't believe you made out with the guy you called

'Brock the dumb jock who lived down the block'!" Alek said accusingly.

"He sounds hot to me," Ethan said.

"Well, he asked if I ever thought about kissing another girl," Becky continued.

"My buddies talk about that all the time," Ethan said. "Straight guys are so predictable."

"And I said no. And he said, 'Even Kate Winslet?' Now, we'd just watched *Titanic*, so as you can imagine, she was very fresh in my mind. I don't think I'm a lesbo, but I said yes, I'd make out with her. And then he started naming all of my other favorite movie stars—Audrey Hepburn, Anne Hathaway, Rachel Weisz— and I said yes to all of them. So I guess I'm either a theoretical bisexual or a major fame whore."

"I can't believe you never told me about Brock," Alek said.

"It happened before we even met, Alek," Becky said. "And I didn't want to intimidate you with my experience."

"Lady, you're speaking wiser than you know." Ethan nodded knowingly.

"Ethan, I tried to break him in for you, but you know how difficult he can be," Becky confided. "When you kissed him, did you find—"

"And I think we've had enough of that," Alek cut in quickly. "Boundaries, okay?"

"I agree. Seeing the two of you nuzzling is making me sick." Becky snapped the DVD case shut, strapped on her skates, and started making her way toward the front door. "Good to meet you, Ethan. I'm sure you'll be seeing me around."

17

ALEK FLOATED THROUGH THE NEXT TWO DAYS, HIS newfound freedom expanding his definition of joy. Instead of finishing his Shakespeare paper for Ms. Imbrie's class, Alek stayed up with Ethan until midnight after Becky left that Thursday. And the next morning, he woke up and ate Cracker Jack for breakfast, washing it down with flat leftover Diet Dr Pepper, before leaving to meet Ethan at the train station for another adventure in the city.

When an unexpected shower caught them eating gelato in the West Village, Ethan ducked into the nearest hotel, explained to the doorman that he was the child of one of the guests, and was rewarded with a beautiful big umbrella that shielded them all the way to the nearest Barnes & Noble. In the bookstore, Ethan showed Alek his favorite urban survival trick. He took an expensive-looking book off one of the shelves, walked around for a while, and then "returned" the book at the cashier.

"We don't usually take items back without receipts, even if they are in perfect condition," the cashier explained.

"It was a gift for my birthday," Ethan explained courteously. A few moments later, he was rewarded with store credit for the amount of the "returned" book.

"You like books, right?" Ethan slid the gift card to Alek, who stared at him in wide-eyed amazement.

As long as Alek continued calling his parents every day and night, they believed that everything was fine.

"What are you going to do today?" his mother asked when he talked to her Saturday morning.

"Who knows, Mom? How're the rest of the families? Did the Kalfayans make you eat their food? How about the Hovanians— have they chilled out at all?"

"Quite the opposite. Nik just had to run out to meet Nanar because there's something she said she needs to tell him."

"You think she's pregnant?" Alek joked.

"That's not funny," his mother responded. "What are you going to do today?"

"I was thinking I'd hit the courts."

"How lovely, Alek. By yourself?"

"No, with a friend."

"What's that?" she asked.

"I said, I'm going with a friend," Alek repeated.

"Sorry, hon—I was talking to your father." Alek could hear his father's muffled voice on the other side of the phone. "Honey, it sounds like something's come up. I'm going to have to call you back, okay?"

"Sure, Mom—see you guys tomorrow. Have a good ride back."

Alek hung up the phone. He flipped through the sections of the Sunday *Times* that arrived on Saturday, like Arts and the *Magazine,* relishing the ability to read them fresh. As the youngest member of his family, he usually had to make do with everyone else's smudged and creased hand-me-downs.

"What time do you think your folks'll be back tomorrow?" Ethan asked.

"Late—they're driving back in one shot."

"Sweet."

"We're playing tennis today," Alek decided, putting down the newspaper.

"I love it when you take charge." Ethan grinned.

"Let's see if you still feel that way after I've demolished you."

When he and Ethan got to the courts, it became clear that Ethan wasn't a tennis player; he just enjoyed trying to get the ball over the net. So Alek held back. Even then, Ethan was impressed.

"I gotta tell you, dude, when you told me that tennis was your jam, I didn't really believe you. But you really got game!"

"You haven't seen anything yet."

"Really?"

Encouraged by Ethan's admiration, Alek began playing his best game, reclaiming his two-handed forehand, slamming the ball down the line for winners, and approaching the net like he had at the peak of his game last year.

"I like playing tennis with you, Ethan," Alek told him as they toweled off after their match.

"Why, because I look so hot on the court?"

"No, you look like an idiot running around trying to return my shots. I like it because it's nice to do something I'm better at."

Ethan playfully flicked his towel at Alek, who playfully flicked his back.

"What's taking you so long?" Alek asked, walking into the kitchen. He surveyed the piles of laundry, unwashed dishes, and bags of garbage, wondering how much time it would take him to restore the house to Khederian-acceptable order.

"One sec!" Ethan called back.

Ethan stood holding two glasses of water, staring at the refrigerator door. Alek took the glasses out of his hands and put them on the counter. Standing behind Ethan, Alek wrapped his hands around Ethan's waist, nuzzling his face against his neck. "What're you looking at?"

"Grim, isn't it?" Ethan was reading the black-and-white photocopies of two newspaper articles taped to the Khederian refrigerator. One headline read, *Tales of Armenian Horrors Confirmed*, and the other read, *Exiled Armenians Starve in the Desert*. A photograph of a caravan of emaciated Armenians on a forced desert march hung next to the article. Since Alek couldn't remember a time when the articles hadn't been on his refrigerator door, his eyes often passed over them.

"These are from the *New York Times*?" Ethan asked.

"Yup—the first article is from 1915. The second one with the photograph is from 1916. That was just the beginning of it."

"I thought you said that some people still deny this ever happened."

"They do," Alek replied simply.

"How? I mean, if people were writing articles about it at the time, how could anyone possibly deny it?"

"And that, Ethan, is the crux of the incredible pain-born-of-injustice that Armenians carry around with them." Alek found that the stories about his family's past were there when he reached for them, like ingredients in a well-stocked pantry. "My parents didn't want us to take what we had for granted, or to forget the atrocities that were inflicted on our people, so they put these articles up here."

"I've got no idea what it must be like to carry that stuff around with you. I'm a European mutt. My dad's Irish, French, and German, but none of it means anything to me."

"What about your mom?" Alek asked.

"What about her?"

"You know, you never talk about her," Alek probed gently. "What does she do?"

"Pot," Ethan replied.

"And does she get paid well to smoke pot for a living?" Alek joked back.

"I'm not kidding. She was a hippie who became a lobbyist for the marijuana industry. She's one of the reasons that it's becoming legal in all of those states out west."

"That's not a job you think of someone's parent having," Alek said.

"Well, she's not your average parent," Ethan admitted. "She just wasn't cut out for the whole stay-at-home-mom thing. Or even the go-to-work-mom thing. That's the reason she bolted."

"Do you miss her?" Alek couldn't imagine his parents separated, or what his childhood would've been like with just one of them.

"All the time. But I'd rather be giving it to the man the way she does than a slave to the system. Anyway, even if she were around, I don't think I'd have a connection to her oppressed Hungarian ancestors the way you do to yours."

"It's not like I think about it all the time, you know."

"Really?"

"It's like this," Alek continued. "You're gay, right, but you don't go around thinking to yourself, 'What am I going to wear today, since I'm gay?' or 'How would a gay person react in this situation?' "

"Course not. Sometimes I go an entire five minutes without thinking about my own gayness."

"I'm being serious. How often do you really think about it?"

"I guess certain situations make me think about it more than others. Like when Remi and I used to hold hands in the mall and get looks. But when I'm walking down the streets of New York City, it doesn't matter."

"Same with being Armenian. Most of the time it's not the top thing on my mind. But I remember Nik coming home from school last year practically in tears because his Modern European History class spent a week on World War I and the teacher never mentioned the Armenians. 'Armenian Genocide' wasn't even a listing in the index at the back of the textbook. When something like that happens, you're forced to figure out what it means to you."

"So that's what it means to you—pain and suffering and loss?"

"Well, that's part of it, sure. But there's lots more, too."

Alek led Ethan to a glass cabinet on the opposite side of the kitchen. He carefully opened it and handed Ethan a large, framed photograph. "This portrait was taken almost a hundred years ago. It's my mom's side of the family, when everyone lived in Van. Van is in Turkey; my family had lived in the Armenian quarter there for almost three hundred years."

"How come they're making those crazy faces? Usually everyone in old pictures has those depressingly serious expressions and are standing totally still."

"You see this?" Alek pointed to a corner of the photograph.

"It looks like a cat's tail," Ethan guessed.

"That's right. You see, the Van cat was this very special thing—they were supposed to be good luck, because they have one blue and one green eye. The second this picture was taken, Sarma, the family cat, leaped in front of the camera and startled everyone. They took another picture, but because this one was considered ruined, they gave it to my great-grandfather. You see him, he's the one in the back row, all the way on the right."

"He looks like he's our age."

"Yeah, he was fifteen," Alek said. "He's the only one who survived the genocide."

Ethan looked at all of the Armenian faces in the photograph—laughing, surprised, annoyed. "Let me get this straight—everyone else in this picture was killed?"

Alek nodded. "I think all the time how lucky I am to be here—how lucky I am that my great-grandfather, against his parents' wishes, picked up and left after things got bad. And took this picture with him, because otherwise, I'd never know what those relatives looked like. But there are lots of other things that come with being Armenian," Alek said, taking the picture back from Ethan and returning it to the glass cabinet. "Like this." He held out a large, round, flat piece of pottery, the size of a dinner plate. Ethan held it up, inspecting the images painted on the surface.

"This was made by the Balian family in the Armenian quarter in Jerusalem. This signature," Alek said, flipping the plate over, "is how you know it's the real thing. They're the only ones who make this stuff anymore."

"There's an Armenian quarter in Jerusalem?"

"Sure. We were the first country to convert to Christianity, you know."

"It's beautiful," Ethan said, admiring the two intertwined fish painted green and brown, framed by an intricate blue border.

"All of the images on Armenian pottery have a meaning. Sometimes they tell a story, or sometimes the image is symbolic."

"What do these two little guys mean?" Ethan asked.

"It means *miasnut'yun*."

"Excuse me?"

"I don't know exactly how it translates into English. Unity? Togetherness? The image means two whole beings, complete unto themselves, that together form a new thing. Something bigger and better."

"Sounds like a good translation to me." Ethan leaned in and kissed Alek.

Later that night, Ethan and Alek sat on Alek's bed, limbs entangled.

"Your room is so neat," Ethan said, somewhere between admiration and disgust.

"We clean every Sunday after church."

"And did your parents choose this puke green for the walls?"

"It's 'moss green,' and my mother says it's calming," Alek said, nodding.

"Our next project should be this room. We should make it over the way we did you," Ethan said.

"One thing at a time," Alek responded. He wondered how his parents were going to react to his new hair and clothes when they came home tomorrow. "What do you want to do tonight?"

"We could watch TV, I guess," Ethan said.

"As long as we don't watch anything with Kim Kardashian. You have no idea how many hours Armenians around the world spend complaining about how she, out of everyone, was chosen to represent us. I actually heard my mother say she missed the good ol' days when Cher would skimp around in inappropriate outfits."

"Did she tell you why she had to get off the phone in such a rush?"

Alek laughed. "I'm guessing she found out that the milk at the hotel's continental breakfast wasn't organic and locally sourced. She called back when we were on the courts, but didn't leave a message because she never does. Then I tried her, but it went straight to voice mail, so I left a message at the hotel. I had to spell 'Khederian' three times."

"What's Cher's last name?" Ethan asked.

"Sarkisian."

"Sarkisian, Khederian, Kardashian—do all Armenian names end in 'ian'?"

"Indeed they do. Or 'yan' sometimes, but it's the same thing. It's the patronymic. You know," Alek said, responding to Ethan's quizzical look, "the equivalent of 'son' in English. You have Johnson and Anderson, we have Hovanian and Boghossian. It just means 'son of' in Armenian."

"You're a treasure trove of facts," Ethan said.

"Of useless Armenian trivia," Alek replied. "We should probably get a head start on cleaning the house."

"You guys don't have a cleaning lady?"

"Are you kidding me? We tried that when my mom started working full time, but my parents spent so much time cleaning the day before she arrived because they wanted to impress her with what a clean house we kept that they figured it wasn't worth it." But when Alek thought about the energy involved in actually detaching from Ethan and then taking out the garbage, loading up the dishwasher, wiping down the counters, vacuuming the carpets, and mopping the floors, it just seemed impossible. "I guess we could just do it tomorrow."

"Nosiree. We have one more NYC trip planned."

"Ethan, my family gets back tomorrow! We don't have time to get into the city before then."

"But you said they weren't coming back until late, right?"

"Yeah."

"So leave the rest to me. Just meet me at the station in time for the 10:17 and we'll be back by dinner. Or better yet, I might just spend the night and we can head out together tomorrow."

"You can be very persuasive, Ethan."

"Tomorrow is a surprise, so don't even think about asking what we're gonna do, okay?"

Thousands of possibilities spun around in Alek's mind like a slot machine. "I don't know what I'm going to do when my parents get back. The idea of not being able to get into New York whenever I want and being stranded in the suburbs again is so depressing."

"You know, I don't think the suburbs are that bad," Ethan said.

"How can you, who introduced me to the city, think that? There's nothing to do here. Ever. Even if you were old enough to have a license and we had a car, then what? We could drive to the mall? Unless it was after eight p.m., of course. Then our only option would be the diner down Route 130. But if we were in the city, we could walk the High Line or get paletas or watch the sun set over the river or get lost in Central Park. We could even play gay soccer with the Ramblers! That's why I hate it here so much. It's like the sun sets and everything dies."

"You really think the suburbs *suck*?"

"Yeah."

"And you think that's a bad thing?"

"Well, how can it be good?"

"Let me show you."

Ethan slid out from behind Alek. He plugged his phone into Alek's speakers, and a Rufus song started pumping out: *"You can go out, dancing . . ."*

" 'Between My Legs,' right?" Alek asked.

"Righter than you could guess," Ethan responded. He turned the volume up, until Alek could feel the bass pulsing in his bones. Ethan closed the door and dimmed the lights until the room was so dark, Alek could barely see him.

"Ethan!"

"Shhhh." Ethan whipped off his shirt, then walked to Alek and put his finger on his lips. Alek kissed the finger lightly. Ethan reached out and put his other hand on Alek's knee. He leaned in, kissing Alek on the face, mouth, and neck, slowly making his way down his body. His hand climbed up the side of Alek's leg, until his fingers rested at the top of his pants. Then they slowly started fumbling with the button. Alek closed his eyes and leaned his head back.

Every inch that Ethan went down made Alek's heart thump a little harder. A few days ago, when Ethan had joked about this right before Becky walked in, Alek was more scared than anything else. He still felt scared, but now he felt like he might be ready, too.

Ethan's hands had succeeded in freeing the button. Alek let Rufus's lyrics wash over him. The song had never made more sense to him. If the world were coming to an apocalyptic, cataclysmic end, this is exactly where he'd want to be: with Ethan.

Alek opened his eyes and found Ethan's looking up at him. He knew the question being asked. Was he ready? Did he want Ethan to do this?

But before Alek could decide, the door to his bedroom swung open violently. A figure holding a golf club above its head, poised to strike, leaped into the room.

"Call the police!" Ethan screamed as he lunged, knocking the figure down to the ground.

Alek jumped over Ethan and the assailant to reach his desk, fumbling with his password-protected cell phone.

"9-1-1," the operator stated crisply in Alek's ear. "What's your emergency?"

Screams erupted as two more people appeared in the doorway, one holding a baseball bat and the other wielding his mother's favorite Le Creuset cast-iron skillet, the one she kept hidden in the front closet. *How would these intruders know how to find that?* Alek wondered. *Unless . . .*

"Stop! No one move!" Alek screamed.

Everyone in the room froze.

"Sorry, ma'am, there's no emergency," Alek said into the phone, hanging up. He flipped on the light, revealing his brother and mother standing in the doorway and Ethan, his fist raised, pinning Alek's dad on the floor.

"Ethan, stop!" Alek yelled, grabbing Ethan's arm before the punch could land. Ethan looked down and quickly scrambled off Mr. Khederian.

"Oh, I'm so sorry, Alek's dad. Are you okay?"

"Of course I'm okay," Alek's dad replied indignantly, rising to his feet. He looked at Alek. "Are *you* okay?"

"Why wouldn't I be?" Alek asked.

"When we got here, the front door was open, and the house was such a mess, I assumed it had been ransacked," his mother explained, putting the skillet down. "We thought we had arrived mid-robbery."

"So you snuck up here to apprehend the burglars?" Alek asked incredulously.

His mother nodded.

"God, you're so baroque! Why didn't you just call the police? What if one of these imaginary robbers had a gun?"

"We did call the police. But we were worried about you," his mother said.

"Why is the house such a mess?" Alek's father demanded. "And what were the two of you doing up here with all the lights off and . . ." His father trailed off. Alek felt his cheeks sting bright red. Everyone in the room stood in awkward silence as Alek's family realized what they'd walked in on.

Everyone except for Ethan, of course, who just sat back on the floor and started laughing.

"You think this is funny, young man?" Alek heard his father say in the low voice he reserved for the worst situations.

"Well, dude—"

"I'm not a dude. I'm an adult. You can call me Mr. Khederian. Although after what I've seen tonight, I doubt you'll ever call me anything again." Now it was Ethan's turn to freeze. Alek had seen Ethan charm himself out of situation after situation, but even his most winning smile was a powerless trinket in the face of an enraged Armenian patriarch. "What's your name?"

"It's, uh . . . uh . . ." Ethan stuttered.

"His name is Ethan Novick," Nik volunteered nervously. "He's in my class at school."

"Mr. Novick, I imagine the police will be arriving within a few minutes. If you're still here by then, I have every intention of telling them you're a trespasser."

"I wasn't trespassing. I'm a friend of Alek's," Ethan protested.

"Unfortunately for you, this is not Alek's house. It's mine. And if you remove yourself from it in the next sixty seconds and I'm confident that I'll never have the displeasure of seeing you here again, there's a chance you won't spend the evening in jail. Am I being perfectly clear?"

Ethan looked at Alek. Alek knew he should say something—that he should stand up for Ethan or explain to his parents that things weren't as bad as they seemed. He knew, at least, that that's what Ethan would do. But instead, he hung his head in silent shame. Even more than his parents' shock, he could feel Ethan's disappointment burn into him.

"Yes, sir," Ethan said, grabbing his shirt and bolting out of the room.

Alek ran out and followed Ethan downstairs to the front door.

"I need to get out of here, man," Ethan said. "I'll see you tomorrow, okay?"

"Ethan, there's no way I'm going to be able to meet you tomorrow."

"Why not?"

"Are you kidding me? My parents are going to kill me. Maybe, if I'm lucky, they'll just ground me until senior year. But the chances of my being free to go into the city tomorrow morning are pretty much the same as my sprouting wings right now and flying there."

"Just crash at my place tonight, then," Ethan offered, his eyes twinkling.

Alek stared at him in disbelief. "You just don't get it, do you?"

"Get what?"

"What it's like to have to do what your parents say."

"You don't *have* to do that, Alek. You *choose* to. Just like you're *choosing* not to meet me tomorrow, even though you know I've planned something special."

"You don't understand, because your dad doesn't care what you do."

"You don't know a thing about my dad," Ethan said sharply. "So don't use him as the excuse for being too much of a pussy to stand up to your folks."

"That's not what I meant," Alek backtracked.

"Whatever," Ethan said. "You better go up to those terrorists who care about you so much they're going to ground you forever. Catch you later, dude." Ethan ran out, slamming the door behind him.

Alek stared at the back of his front door stupidly for a second, then slowly climbed the stairs back up to his room.

"Aleksander Khederian, you have so much explaining to do that I don't even know where you're going to begin," his mother said when he reappeared in the doorway to his room.

"I didn't think you guys were coming home until tomorrow." Alek felt the tears rising up in his eyes. "If you guys would just let me explain—"

"I don't think I need an explanation for what I just saw," his father told him. "You're a disgrace to this family."

The blood drained out of Alek's face, and he exhaled sharply, as if he'd been punched in the stomach. His hands started shaking, and he leaned against the door frame to his bedroom. He looked at Nik, impossibly hoping that his brother would stand up for him, or even just say something. But Nik looked away, shaking his head in disbelief.

"Alek, before you go to sleep tonight, you will clean the entire house, top to bottom," his father said. "Tomorrow morning at eight a.m., you will come to the dining room, where your mother and I will discuss this week's events. After the day we just had, all we wanted was to come back home and get some rest. I can't tell you how disappointed I am that you've denied us even that. We expect full honesty and full disclosure. Have I made myself clear?"

"Yes, Dad." Alek dropped his head and waited for the rest of his family to leave his room.

18

AT 7:55 THE NEXT MORNING, ALEK WALKED INTO THE dining room and sat down at the table. He stifled a yawn. Cleaning the house had kept him up later than he was used to, and he knew this wasn't the time to cut corners. Not only had he thrown all the trash away, but he even took the recycling out and scrubbed the kitchen down, using an old toothbrush to get into the hard-to-reach corners. Then he emptied the refrigerator so he could wipe it clean, which he knew was his mom's least favorite task, because of how she worried about the food going bad at room temperature.

When he finally got to bed, he was too anxious to fall asleep. He lay awake staring up at the ceiling, his mind racing and his heart pounding, until he finally drifted into a restless slumber. When he woke up in the morning, he couldn't remember the nightmares he had had, only the bizarre impressions they'd left.

The sound of his parents walking down the stairs caused Alek to sit up straight. They entered the dining room and sat opposite him, in front of the credenza that stored the family's good china and silverware.

His mother looked especially formidable, dressed in the power suit that meant she'd be going into work this Sunday. His father was wearing a button-down shirt tucked into crisp brown pants, a formal departure from the sweats he usually wore since he'd been laid off. Alek was suddenly able to imagine what it would be like to meet them in a work environment: not as his warm, providing parents, but as serious, educated, driven professionals.

"Aleksander, when we left you alone last Monday, it was an act of trust and respect. In so blatantly violating the guidelines that we set down, you disrespected us and you shattered that trust," his mother began.

"But I didn't—" Alek interjected.

"That's enough," she cut him off immediately. "We will make it clear when we want a response from you, and when we don't. This is an instance of the latter."

"Yes, Mom." He looked over to his father, who met Alek's gaze blankly, his face a stone mask.

"We'll start with the thing that upsets us most," his mother continued.

"I know what you're going to say, and I think it really sucks," Alek jumped in. "You guys are totally homophobic. If you had walked in on Nik and Nanar making out, there's no way you'd react like this."

"We're not talking about Nik, and we're most certainly not talking about Nanar," his father exploded. "Besides, Nik is almost seventeen, and this is about you. Now. At fourteen. And if you think you and that boy are what upset us the most, you don't give us nearly enough credit."

Alek faltered. "What do you mean?"

"You know your mother and I met while we were living in New York. Don't you think we had any gay friends?" his dad asked incredulously.

"I guess I didn't think—"

"You can say that again," his father muttered.

Alek's mom gently put her arm on her husband's shoulder. "Alek, you remember Tim?"

"Uncle Timmy, dad's roommate?"

"Yes, well, Uncle Timmy was my first boyfriend in college. He came out right after we broke up."

"Uncle Timmy is gay? Why didn't you ever tell us?"

"I suppose it felt easier not to. But I wish you had as much faith in us as we usually do in you. We brought you and Nik up to be open-minded, and I think that's the least you can expect from us."

"So you don't care if I'm gay?"

"Of course I care. I am your mother. I care about anything that happens to you. And if it were up to me, would I pick you being gay?" Alek's mom's voice broke. She paused for a second, weighing the question and the implications of her answer. "To be honest, I probably wouldn't. But I'm saying that because I saw how hard it was for my gay friends to come to terms with their sexuality, in the aftermath of the AIDS crisis, to live in a world that wasn't thrilled to have them. And even though I think it's better now, I hate the idea of my baby having to deal with any more pain in this world than he already has to." Alek's mom paused again, tears welling in her eyes. Then, with surprising ferocity, she said, "And if you think this excuses you from providing me grandchildren, you couldn't be more mistaken."

"Um, and how exactly do you expect me to do that?" Alek asked.

"You'll figure it out," his mother informed him.

"You can adopt. Lots of gay couples do that," his father said.

"I know, I know," Alek responded, still trying to absorb this unexpected turn of events.

"Then we'll continue." Mrs. Khederian produced an envelope from her briefcase. Alek recognized it as one of the pieces of mail he'd gathered during his parents' trip. "Can you explain this to us, Alek?"

Alek stared at her stupidly for a second.

"This is one of the times that we would like a response," his mom prodded.

Alek picked up the envelope. Inside was a mcmo from the school, listing his absences.

"This is what upsets you most?"

"You know how important education is in this house," his mom stated.

Alek had spent all night and morning dreading this meeting with his parents. It had consumed him as he was cleaning up the house. It had kept him awake late in the night, and when he was finally able to fall asleep, it haunted his nightmares.

But now he relaxed. He knew that the rest of this meeting was going to be difficult and uncomfortable. He knew he'd have a lot of apologizing to do, and that it would take time before things were normal again. But he realized his parents were behaving exactly the way he should've expected: putting academics before everything else.

"I cut school to go into New York with Ethan," Alek confessed.

"Is that where you got your hair butchered? In New York?" his mother asked.

"Well, yes, but that was a different day."

"So we're going to add going to New York unchaperoned to your list of offenses," his dad said.

"Yes, Dad."

"And what about the second cut—the afternoon period on the twenty-ninth?"

"I got into a fight with Ethan, so I went to the Dairy Queen to find Becky."

"And why weren't we notified about any of these absences?"

"I forged a note from Dad," Alek said, looking away.

His father shook his head in disbelief.

"And so we add forging your father's signature and, worst of all, lying to us."

"Yes," Alek mumbled. When he was performing these individual acts, they hadn't seemed especially deceitful. But when they were laid out bare like this, Alek had to admit they formed an impressive litany.

"Is there anything else you want to tell us?"

"Um, I sorta didn't hand in an English paper on Friday because Ethan and I went into New York again."

"And let me guess—you were planning on forging another note?" his father demanded.

Alek nodded yes.

"Your father and I spent all night wondering how you could behave in a way that was so irresponsible and immature and so, well, unlike you. The only thing that we can attribute your behavior to is this boy, Ethan. He must be a bad influence. The Alek I know would never have done any of those things." His mom folded the paper back up and returned it to its envelope.

Alek's parents exchanged a glance before his mom spoke again. "We don't think you should see him again."

"Are you kidding me?" Alek started choking up. "You spend all this time telling me how you're not homophobic, and now you're telling me that I can't see Ethan anymore? Mom, Dad, please. Punish me as much as you want. Double my chore load until I'm a hundred. Ground me until I go to college. But don't tell me I can't see Ethan."

"Alek, I know this is hard, but it's for your own good," his father insisted.

"You guys are total hypocrites!"

Alek's father looked at him, the anger flaring in his eyes. "Don't insult us, you disrespectful liar," he snapped. "Alek, do you know what it feels like when your child lies to you? And I'm not even talking about anything big. Even a little lie hurts when it comes from someone you love so much. And then to have a parade of lies pour out of your mouth. I hope you do have children, so that one day you can know what it means to be hurt by them in this way. This is not the kind of man we've brought you up to be. You should feel ashamed of yourself. I know that I feel ashamed of you."

"Alek, that's all we have to say," his mom concluded. "Until further notice, consider yourself grounded. You will come home directly after school. Your phone privileges, including your cell phone, are suspended until further notice. We're putting a password on your computer so that you won't be able to access the Internet. You have two more weeks of school left in session. I suggest you pull yourself together and try to salvage this summer."

"Can I say something now?" Alek asked his parents quietly.

"No. Until you start acting like an adult, there's no reason for us to treat you like one."

Alek's parents rose and left the dining room. Alek looked down and saw the damp spots that his tears had made on the place mat.

19

IF THE LAST WEEK OF ALEK'S LIFE HAD BEEN PURE bliss, this one was pure hell. He wasn't even entrusted to walk to school—his father insisted on dropping him off and picking him up. Alek sat in the passenger's seat each morning in silence, daring his father to say something about Alek's Housing Works clothes. But he didn't. The routine of home, school, home, chores, and homework became so entrenched that any other kind of existence felt like a distant memory. The near-perfect tennis weather just made it worse, teasing him from his dad's car. His racket lay in the front closet neglected, like a forgotten friend. He couldn't even see or call Becky.

And the worst thing was that he still hadn't talked to Ethan since their fight. Although Alek wished he could've gone to New York with Ethan that Sunday, the more he'd thought about it, the angrier he'd gotten. Ethan knew that it wasn't his choice. It's not like he *wanted* to get grounded.

By the time Alek slinked to the cafeteria the Monday after his parents had punished him, he had decided that Ethan had been the immature one, and Alek wasn't sure if he was going to sit next to him. Today, Alek thought to himself, Ethan's backpack could be his lunchtime companion.

Alek's plan was preempted when he saw Ethan wasn't sitting at his table. Alek stood in the middle of the cafeteria, getting angrier. *He* was the one who had been humiliated in front of his parents. *He* was the one who had had a door slammed in his face. *He* was the one who was grounded for the rest of his life. *He* was the one who had been stuck in the suburbs while Ethan got to go to New York. And was he supposed to think that it was just a coincidence that Ethan was late today and didn't save him a seat? Did Ethan think he was going to sit at the Dropouts' table by himself? Alek stomped to his old empty table, plopped down on one of the seats, took out his spinach buregs, and propped open his algebra book.

A few minutes later, Alek spied Ethan entering the cafeteria with Josh, Jack, and Pedro. When Ethan saw Alek, he stopped and whispered to his friends, who beelined to their table, leaving Ethan alone. He stood, looking at Alek from across the room, a blank expression covering his face. Alek looked back past the open pages of his textbook.

Their eyes and stances remained locked, like cowboys in a Western, neither willing to make the first move or back down. After a few of these infinite moments, Alek broke the standstill by turning back to his book. *If he isn't man enough to come over and apologize, I'd rather prepare for Algebra,* Alek thought to himself. A few minutes later, Alek cheated a glance at Ethan. Instead of being in his usual seat, Ethan was sitting on the other side of the table, his back turned to Alek.

After he finished his lunch, Alek walked into his Algebra classroom and went directly to Mr. Weedin's desk. Mr. Weedin put down the newspaper he'd been reading and looked down his glasses at Alek. "Can I help you?" he asked.

"Mr. Weedin, I'm having trouble seeing the chalkboard from the back of the room," Alek lied, "and I was wondering if I could move up for the remaining two weeks of class."

"That seems reasonable enough. You can take that seat," Mr. Weedin said, pointing to the desk in the front row farthest from the door.

The easy part's done, Alek thought to himself.

"Is there anything else, Mr. Khederian?"

"I know that you have a policy to fail anyone who cuts a class unexcused, and I wanted to see if there was any extra credit that I could do to try to make up for my absence last Friday. I really don't want to fail."

"Does that mean that your absence last Friday, unlike your earlier absences this semester, was *un*excused?" Mr. Weedin asked.

"It does," Alek admitted.

"Mr. Khederian, you clearly have a strong grip on this material, and if you hadn't cut, I would've considered recommending you for the Honor Track next year. But I'm afraid that I can't go around making exceptions for students, regardless of how bright they appear." Mr. Weedin picked up his paper and continued reading.

His teacher's resolution almost made Alek give up. But he

knew how important this was for his parents. And, he had to admit, for himself as well.

"Mr. Weedin, don't you think failing me in a class when you think I'm capable of delivering Honor Track material is counterproductive?" Alek cleared his throat. " 'Let us once lose our oaths to find ourselves, / Or else we lose ourselves to keep our oaths.' "

"Is that Shakespeare?" Mr. Weedin asked, intrigued.

"Yeah, it's from *Love's Labour's Lost*. I just wrote an essay comparing and contrasting that play to *Romeo and Juliet* in English, and that quote really stuck in my head."

"Why?" Mr. Weedin leaned back and slid his glasses down so he could peer at Alek unobstructed.

"I guess I feel like we spend so much time trying to keep the promises we make, or the rules we set up, but it's also important to look at those promises and rules and make sure they're actually doing what we want them to do, and not the other way around."

"Well, Mr. Khederian, you make a persuasive case." Mr. Weedin tapped his pencil against his desk three times. "I'm not going to make it easy for you. For the remainder of the class, I'm going to double your homework load. If you complete it all satisfactorily, then I will reduce the penalty from failing to dropping your grade one full letter. So the highest grade you could receive would be a B."

Alek had to stop himself from hugging Mr. Weedin. "Thank you, Mr. Weedin, thank you so, so much. I promise that I'll do my best."

"What is your best, I wonder?"

"I don't know, Mr. Weedin, but I'm looking forward to finding out."

"Me too, Alek."

Alek scurried to his new seat, took out his homework and textbook, and made sure to be inspecting them intently when Ethan entered the class. Alek hoped Ethan would be surprised to see Alek sitting on the other side of the classroom.

Confined to his home, Alek actually welcomed the increase in his homework load. He just wished that his parents could dock his grade, the way Ms. Imbrie had told him she'd do when he handed in the Shakespeare paper that morning, and then move on, instead of looking at him with hurt and disappointment every time they were forced to interact with him.

The next Saturday morning, Alek got up just before nine a.m. and tiptoed downstairs to get to the *New York Times* before anyone else in the family woke up.

As he was putting down the *Magazine* an hour later, Nik walked in.

"Mind if I read with you?" he asked. They were the first words Nik had spoken to him since the family had arrived from their vacation a week ago.

Alek shrugged his shoulders indifferently.

Nik sat next to Alek, picking up the discarded *Magazine* as Alek made his way through Arts, Sports, and the front page. They sat reading for another hour in silence. When Alek finished International News, he put down his folded section and got up to go back to his room.

"Alek, you have a sec?" Nik asked.

"Nik, if you're going to give me crap for something I did or didn't do, save it. I don't have the energy."

"You don't have to be hostile."

"Really? Don't I? This whole week has been hell, Nik. You've never been grounded, even for a day, so you wouldn't understand. Isn't the older sibling supposed to be the one who screws up so it's easier for the younger one?"

"What?"

"Do you realize how hard it is to be your brother? You do everything right. You get perfect grades, you work as a camp counselor during the summers, you're never late for breakfast or dinner, and you're in the church youth group, for God's sake. I wish you did one thing—*any*thing—that Mom and Dad didn't approve of."

"Are you kidding me?" Nik asked.

"Do I sound like I'm kidding?"

"Alek, you've got it all wrong. Being the oldest one sucks. Do you think I like the burden of feeling like I have to do the right thing all the time? Do you know how many times Mom or Dad tells me that they're counting on me, Andranik, firstborn, and that I can't let them down?"

"Then why do you always do what they say? And what they expect? You're even dating an Armenian, for God's sake!"

"Not anymore."

"What?"

Nik looked around to make sure they were alone. "Did Mom and Dad tell you why we came back early from our trip?"

"Honestly, with everything that happened, I didn't feel like

219

changing vacation plans was on the very short list of things I'm allowed to talk to them about."

"I'm sure that wasn't the reception you would've planned if you had been expecting us," Nik said pointedly.

"Not in the least," Alek agreed.

"Well, it turns out Nanar isn't really Armenian. Or at least, not *just* Armenian," Nik confided. "The day before the vacation was supposed to end, she told me that she'd learned something that she thought I should know."

"What could it possibly be?"

"Well, her dad is Armenian, but her mom isn't. She's Turkish!"

Alek's jaw dropped. "So that means . . ."

"Nanar is half-Armenian, half-Turkish. When her mom and dad fell in love, they knew his parents would never accept her. So they lied about it and have been lying about it ever since."

"How did Nanar find out?"

"It started with the heritage project we were doing for Armenian Youth. She started digging into her mom's family history, and the more she dug, the shadier things got. Even before we left on the trip, she told me she felt like her mom was hiding something from her. Then we were doing research at the library in Burlington, and she found a census from the town where her parents were born. Her father's family was listed on the Armenian side, but her mom was listed with the Turks! She confronted her parents and they confessed, and she came running to tell me."

"What did you do, Nik?"

Nik looked away.

"Oh, no," Alek said.

"I told her I couldn't date someone Turkish," Nik admitted, looking away in shame. "And then I ran and told Mom and Dad, who told the rest of the families, and one by one, everyone decided to go home from the vacation early. The Kalfayans didn't even wait for Nanar and her parents. They just packed up and left. I don't even know how they got home."

"Nik, you have done some stupid things in your life, but I have to say, this one really takes the baklava. Your girlfriend, the only person you're actually bearable around, outs herself to you, and you reject her? She didn't have to tell you. She could've just kept her secret to herself, but she decided to be honest with you. Do you know how much courage that takes? Is there something about being straight that makes you insensitive, or is it just a cosmic coincidence?"

"Don't you think I know that I acted like a jerk?" Nik asked, anguished. "Even when I was doing it, I felt it wasn't right."

"Then why did you?"

"I knew it was what Mom and Dad would've wanted," Nik confessed. "But now, I don't care. Being without Nanar, I feel like a dolma without its stuffing. Like a baklava without its pis-tachios. Like a—"

"Okay, I get it," Alek cut him off.

"I need to figure out a way to get her back."

"Even if it means pissing off Mom and Dad?"

"Even then," Nik swore. "Is that what being apart from Ethan is like for you?"

"It's not the same thing, because Nanar didn't do anything wrong, unlike Ethan. He hasn't talked to me since that day."

"And have you tried to talk to him?" Nik asked.

Alek looked away rather than responding.

"At least I know when I'm being an idiot," Nik said. "Can you imagine what it must've been like for him? Meeting Mom and Dad would be traumatic under normal circumstances. *You* have to reach out to *him*, Alek."

Alek felt that sinking feeling inside that he got when he was wrong and someone else was right. And that feeling started morphing into something else, something wild and dangerous and crazy. "I think I know what we need to do," Alek said.

"You do?"

"Yes. Something that will win Nanar back for you, fix things with Ethan for me, and get Mom and Dad off our backs. But that's only if it works, of course."

"And if it doesn't?"

"Then Nanar and Ethan will never speak to you and me again, and Mom and Dad will ground us both until the Turks finally admit to the Armenian Genocide."

"Where do I sign up?"

"You really up for this?"

"I trust you, Alek. Think about how long we've been working against each other. If we actually started working together, what can't we do?"

20

"YOU'RE ROLLING THE SARMA TOO TIGHT," ALEK insisted.

"Am not," Nik said.

"They're going to burst when they're cooking," Alek warned.

"Will not."

"Will too."

"Will not!" Nik practically screamed, ripping the leaf he'd been working on, sending lamb and rice stuffing flying all over the kitchen.

The brothers Khederian paused for a moment and took deep breaths.

"Why don't you do it with me?" Nik asked.

"You know Mom and Dad haven't taught me how yet," Alek responded.

"So I will. Here," Nik said, passing one of the unwrapped grapevine leaves to his brother.

"Really?"

"Why not? Put around a tablespoon of the stuffing in the middle, fold in the sides, then roll it up from the bottom."

Alek accepted the leaf and got to work, following his brother's instructions.

"You see how much faster it goes if we do it together?" Nik said. Alek nodded in agreement, enjoying the long-awaited feeling of the grapevine leaf in his hand.

"Alek, after we finish rolling the sarma, I'll start chopping the onions for the string beans and lentils."

He placed the completed leaf in the pot, starting a second layer on top of the already-rolled leaves.

"Why don't you start on the lahmajoun and I'll do the onions?"

Alek surveyed the family kitchen, which looked like a war zone. Nik had gotten one of his friends from student council to take him shopping for the ingredients that morning. They had returned hours ago, which Alek and Nik had naïvely believed would give them more than enough time to do the cooking, and laid out each ingredient neatly as they'd seen their parents do before embarking on a great meal-making. Between then and now, however, it looked like an earthquake had rumbled through the kitchen, violently tossing the ingredients in random directions. And not a single dish was ready.

"What time is it?" Alek asked nervously.

"Seven fifteen."

"That only leaves us forty-five minutes!"

"Then what're you waiting for?"

Alek chopped his anxiety out on the onions. When he had suggested the dinner party to Nik last week, it had seemed like the perfect idea. They had spent the rest of that Saturday and all the next Sunday flipping through their parents' cookbooks, trying to put together the perfect meal.

"What about making kufteh for the appetizer?" Alek had asked his brother.

"What's that again?"

"Can there possibly be some piece of Armenian culture you don't know?" Alek asked, faux-shocked.

"Just tell me what it is."

"Aunt Arsinee makes it every Easter, remember? It's that lamb/pine nut/parsley patty thing, like an Armenian slider. She makes it with lots of cumin."

"Isn't that really hard to make? I think we need to make things that we know how to do. Or at least things that we think we can pull off."

Alek considered this. "Good point, Nik," he conceded.

They had agreed to start with premade lahmajoun instead, a thin flatbread baked with ground meat and herbs that simply needed to be heated up. For the entrée, they had decided to make the sarma, which would be accompanied by bulgur, lentils, and green beans in a walnut sauce.

If he had realized how much chopped onion the green beans needed, Alek might've selected a different dish. He tried to look away while chopping to protect his eyes from watering, but was worried that he'd end up cutting his fingers.

"Here, let me show you a trick," Nik offered. He lit a candle from the dining room and placed it next to the chopping board. "That should do it."

"Really?" Alek asked.

"Yeah, cutting onions makes you cry because enzymes from the surface mix with the sulfenic acids inside to produce syn-propanethial-S-oxide. The gas floats up to your eyes, reacting with the moisture to create sulfuric acid. Then your eyes burn, releasing more water, and a chain reaction forms. But the flame draws the gas away, preempting it."

"I can't believe I'm actually happy you're a nerd for once," Alek said.

"Just chop those onions, okay? T-minus thirty minutes." Nik filled a large pot of water, put it on the range, and turned the flame to high. "Let's see," he thought out loud. "That's probably two gallons of water, and at a minute a quart, I'm going to guess it'll boil in around ten minutes."

"Your sorta cool nerdiness just descended into uncool super-nerdiness, FYI," Alek informed him. He took a large skillet for the green beans and put it on medium-low heat. Once the skillet was warm, he poured in a few tablespoons of olive oil, waited for it to start shimmering, then dumped half the onions in, gently stirring them until they were translucent. While the onions cooked, he pounded the walnuts and garlic into a paste, then seasoned it with coriander, paprika, salt, cayenne, and red wine vinegar.

"I'm going to start the lentils," Nik said, putting a pot on low heat. He waited for it to warm up, then added a few tablespoons of olive oil. He took the remaining onions and dumped them inside, letting them cook slowly until they caramelized, as he'd seen his dad do a million times. While the onions quietly sizzled, he gave the lentils a thorough rinse and began sifting through, looking for stones or debris.

"Good call," Alek commended him. "Can you imagine the fuss Mom would make if she bit into something hard and inedible? It's almost enough reason to slip one onto her plate to see what happens."

"Almost," Nik said, making sure Alek was kidding. "You never told me how you got Ethan to come, by the way."

Alek laughed nervously, then removed the trimmed green beans from the fridge and tossed them in with the translucent onions in the large skillet.

"He *is* going to be here, isn't he, Alek?"

"Sure."

"So what's that nervous giggle about?" Nik asked.

"It's just that, well, I spent the last week trying to get the courage up to ask him—" Alek began.

"Which is your way of telling me that it didn't actually happen, right?" Nik continued.

"So I had a friend do it for me," Alek finished.

Alek's dad had another job interview and hadn't been able to pick him up after school on Friday, so Alek had taken a detour to Becky's house on the way home. He had knocked on the door urgently, praying that Becky would be home. He was supposed to call his dad's cell phone from the landline after school, so his window was only a few minutes wide.

"Where have you been, dumb-ass?" she had asked him when she opened the door. "You haven't returned any of my calls. Or e-mails. Or texts. Or smoke signals."

"I'm grounded for life. My parents walked in on me and Ethan."

"I wonder if I should start a support group with them. I was totally traumatized when it happened to me."

"Thanks, Becky."

"Always here for you."

"Look, I need you to do something for me." He rushed through the explanation of everything that had happened. "That's why I need you to carry a message for me and ask Ethan to come over for dinner tomorrow night with my family."

"Are you Romeo or Juliet?" she asked.

"What?"

"Well, if I have to be the Nurse, ferrying messages back and forth between the two of you, I want to know who's who."

"I'm going to have to tell you I'm Juliet for you to do this for me, aren't I?"

"You're quick."

"Okay, Becky. If you're the Nurse, then Ethan is Romeo and I'm Juliet."

"Say it again."

"I'm Juliet," Alek repeated.

"Leave it to me. He'll be there," Becky had reassured him.

"And make sure he knows what he's in for, okay?" Alek had told her.

Alek looked at his brother, who was giving the lentils one final pass. "How did you get Nanar to agree to come over?"

"I did what any self-respecting guy would do. I returned all the Armenian books I bought this summer and used that money to have a dozen roses delivered to her house with a note begging for her forgiveness and telling her that if she took me back, I'd be her slave forever."

"Very masculine."

"It worked, okay?"

Alek let the pot with boiling water cool down for a few minutes, and then gently poured half of it into the pot with the uncooked, rolled-up sarma. He turned the flame to medium-high, and the moment the water started boiling again, covered the pot and dropped the heat down to medium, letting the dish cook at a gentle rolling boil. The rich, earthy smell of grapevine leaves wafted from the pot.

"I don't think I'll ever be able to smell sarma without thinking of home," Nik said.

"I know what you mean," Alek agreed.

Nik's onions had finally caramelized into a crispy dark brown. He poured a few cups of the rinsed lentils into the pot, stirring them around to coat them in the remaining oil. "Now, you know not to put salt in with lentils until after they've finished cooking, right?" Nik instructed.

"Duh," Alek responded. "I'm not one of *these Americans*. Everyone knows you can't put salt or vinegar in with legumes until they're already done or they'll never cook through all the way."

"You know, I don't mean to imply that you're stupid when I tell you things. I'm just trying to be a good older brother," Nik said.

Alek felt thousands of possible sarcastic responses journey from his brain to his tongue. But instead of releasing any of them, he just mumbled "Thanks" under his breath and continued stirring.

"Let's see," Nik said. "The bulgur just needs to sit in there and finish absorbing the water, the sarma has to finish cooking—"

"Don't forget to put the tomato paste in."

"I won't. We've got to finish up the beans, pour the chicken stock into the lentils and let them simmer, put out the madzoon sauce, and heat up the lahmajoun, but I want to wait until the last minute to do that so that it's still warm. I think I can do all that. You want to set the table?"

"Sounds good," Alek said. "I can also put the hors d'oeuvres out."

"Do you really think we need the string cheese as well as the soojoukh? It might be enough just to have the meat out with the pita and olives."

"The string cheese is a must, okay?"

"Okay," Nik conceded.

Alek grabbed the soojoukh, a salted, air-dried meat, from one of the bags and sliced it thinly, then arranged it on a small platter around an impressive serving of the braided cheese. Then he cut the pita into quarters, drained the olives out of their plastic container into a ceramic bowl, and grabbed another small bowl for the pits. He set all the dishes in the living room with a neat stack of napkins nearby.

In the dining room, Alek opened the credenza his parents used to store the nice china and removed a stack of plates. He placed them around the dining room table, then folded six linen napkins and put them on the center of each plate. Next, Alek removed the silverware from the drawers. Since he and Nik had decided against a salad or soup course, he only needed two forks, one knife, and two spoons. Each utensil was placed precisely: appetizer fork then entrée fork on the left side of the plate, knife and teaspoon on the right side of the plate. He laid the dessert spoons horizontally on top, the handles facing right.

When he placed the last spoon, the timer bell on the toaster oven chimed from the kitchen.

"Is that the lahmajoun?" Alek called to his brother.

"Yup," Nik called back. "Do you know where the oven mitts are?"

"I put them back in their drawer."

"Thanks."

Alek went back into the kitchen and took the yogurt dip they had made earlier that day from the refrigerator, sprinkling freshly chopped mint on top.

"Great idea to serve the lahmajoun with madzoon on the side, Nik," Alek complimented his brother.

"Nanar says that's the way her family does it because they love to dip it into the madzoon. When we were hanging out last night, she also told me—" Nik cut himself off when he heard the front door open.

"Are we allowed to come in yet?" their mother called out.

Alek and Nik looked at each other and nodded.

"Come on in, guys," Alek called out. They heard the front door close.

"Boys, everything smells lovely," their father called out warmly. Alek and Nik took off their aprons and walked out of the kitchen to meet their parents in the dining room. Mrs. Khederian was wearing a short, dark blue cotton dress. Alek realized it was the first time all summer he had seen her wearing something other than a suit. Mr. Khederian wore a jacket and tie and square silver cuff links.

"Now, are you going to tell us why you decided to cook us this meal, or will we find out soon enough anyway?" their father asked.

The sound of the doorbell ringing saved them from having to respond.

"Should I get that?" his mother asked.

"No!" the boys called out in unison. Alek looked at the clock in the living room, which read eight o'clock exactly.

"That must be Ethan," he whispered to Nik.

"There's no way an Armenian *or* a Turk would ever be on time," Nik agreed. "You want to get it? I can keep them occupied."

"Thanks," Alek said gratefully.

"Ready?" his brother asked him.

"Ready as I'll ever be," Alek responded.

21

ETHAN WAS WEARING A CREAM LINEN SUIT OVER A
sharply starched white shirt, his hair combed and slicked back.
Alek inhaled his sweet scent, and his knees buckled slightly.
They stood staring at each other, familiar and awkward.

"I didn't actually know if you were going to show up or not,"
Alek said finally.

"Me neither," Ethan admitted.

"Then why did you?" Alek asked.

"Because I'm older."

"What does that have to do with it?"

"I have to be the mature one and forgive you when we fight."

"That's funny, I don't remember asking for your forgiveness."

"And that's what makes my forgiveness so incredibly mature."
Ethan smiled.

The smile warmed Alek's insides. He stepped toward Ethan,
slowly wrapping his hands around his waist. When Ethan didn't

pull away, he leaned his head in, letting it rest against Ethan's chest, and listened to the sound of Ethan's heartbeat.

"I'm so happy you're here," Alek whispered to him.

"Me too," Ethan whispered back, running his hands through Alek's hair.

"You're going to mess it up," Alek protested weakly, staying exactly where he was.

"So, what's the deal, Polly-O?"

"Dinner party—me, you, my bro, his half-Turkish girlfriend, and my folks. Think you can handle it?"

"Becky filled me in. I'm game."

"Let's see if you still feel that way at the end of the night." He took Ethan by the arm and led him inside. His parents were munching on the hors d'oeuvres when Alek returned. They stood up the moment they saw Ethan.

"Mom, Dad, I think you remember Ethan Novick. Ethan, my parents; and I think you know my brother, Nik."

"Mr. and Mrs. Khederian, I want to apologize for our first meeting, which I believe occurred under rather unfortunate circumstances," Ethan recited formally.

"Young man—" Mr. Khederian began.

"Please, sir," Ethan gently interrupted him. "I'd really like to get through this, since I went to the trouble of writing it out and memorizing it." Ethan paused, asking permission, and Mr. Khederian gave the slightest nod of his head. "I want you to know that I care about your son very much, and I hope you give me the opportunity to show you who I really am. I might not be a model citizen like Alek, but that's one of the things I like about him, and I don't want to change that. I don't want to be a bad influence."

Ethan looked at Alek for a second, then continued. "Someone very important to me once said that apologies are cheap. It's easy to say 'I'm sorry' and expect everything to be better. He also said that gifts are better. They say 'I'm sorry, and I'm willing to spend some time and effort to show you how sorry I really am.' So here." Ethan pulled out a small package exquisitely wrapped in white tissue paper from his inside jacket pocket. "Please accept this gift as a token of my apology. I hope you like it."

Alek's father only hesitated for a moment before he held out his hand and took the package from Ethan. He slowly undid the intricate pale green bow, opened the box, and held up its contents: a single ceramic tile of authentic blue-and-white Armenian pottery.

"How did you find this?" Mr. Khederian asked, dumbfounded.

"Peter Balakian gave it to my dad."

"Your dad knows Peter Balakian! That's so cool," Nik exclaimed.

"They've been friends since they went to NYU together. My dad was having lunch with him the day after you got back from your trip early—that's why I wanted Alek to come into the city with me."

"Your father is a professor, then?" Alek's mom asked hopefully.

"Sociology. He specializes in urbanization."

"How lovely, Ethan. What a truly thoughtful and meaningful gift." Mrs. Khederian smiled. Alek's parents looked at each other for a moment. Alek couldn't see any gestures that indicated communication between them, but somehow he knew that an entire conversation transpired in that moment. "I understand Aleksander invited you for dinner tonight?"

"He did, yes," Ethan said, nodding.

"Well, why don't you stay? Tonight. This one time," Mr. Khederian said, extending his hand.

Ethan exhaled visibly, shaking Mr. Khederian's hand. "Thank you, sir. Yes, I'd be honored."

"We have hors d'oeuvres on the coffee table," Nik called in from the living room.

Alek took Ethan's hand and led him into the living room.

"I didn't know your name was short for Aleksander. I'm going to call you 'the Great' from now on," Ethan teased, tussling Alek's spiky hair with his fingers.

"That's a great idea," Alek said. "If you want me to kill you."

"These are authentic Arabic pickles," Nik said, explaining the offerings to Ethan. "And this is—"

"String cheese!" Ethan said gleefully.

"You eat it like this," Nik offered, holding up a braid.

"I got it, man—when it comes to string cheese, I'm a pro." Ethan expertly unbraided a strand and popped it in his mouth.

The doorbell rang for the second time that evening. Alek and Nik looked at each other, then Nik got up and opened the door. He stepped outside and drew Nanar into a fierce embrace. She was wearing a lavender linen dress with a simple matching belt, an off-white shawl hanging from her shoulders. Her heels made her look even taller than she was, and Alek saw a defiant strength in her stance. Rather than apologizing for her height, she was owning it.

"No!" Alek heard his mother say. She crossed to the entry foyer, barricading the would-be guest from entering.

"No what?" Nik asked, disengaging from Nanar but still holding her hand.

"Your mother is saying, 'No, don't ask us to accept her into our house,' " Mr. Khederian said. "And I agree."

"Mr. and Mrs. Khederian, am I so different now from the person who had lunch with you every week after church for the last year?" Nanar asked evenly.

"Yes! Yes, you are!" Mrs. Khederian responded.

"But I've done nothing!" Nanar protested. "Why does finding out that my mother is Turkish make me any crueler or pettier? Why does your opinion of me change because of something I have no control over?"

"Nik told us your family was from Van. Did you know that's where my family was from, too?" Mrs. Khederian asked.

"I didn't," Nanar said.

"Boghos, bring me the picture," Mrs. Khederian said.

"Do you think—" he started, but she cut him off.

"I said bring it to me," his wife insisted, and he left for the kitchen.

"My grandfather was the only person in my family who had the wherewithal to flee Turkey. It's easy to look back and ask, 'Why didn't everyone run when they saw their friends and families persecuted and executed?' But how many of us, even now, would have the courage to leave everything we know, to abandon our roots and our community for a new, foreign world where we didn't speak the language? He was barely older than Nik when he left."

Mr. Khederian returned from the kitchen, holding the botched family portrait. He handed it to his wife, who held it up to Nanar.

"This picture was what my grandfather used to teach me the names of all the family members who were killed in the genocide." She pointed to a woman in the back row, laughing. "Manushag, my grandfather's aunt, who was dragged from her bed in the middle of the night, raped, and then murdered in the town square." She pointed to a man next to her, standing solemnly and proudly in his three-piece suit. "Her husband, Simon, was bayoneted in the stomach when he tried to intervene, and forced to watch, the life slowly leaking out of him." She pointed to four children, standing in height order. "Taniel, Garnik, Adrine, and Sevoug, their kids, were rounded up like animals and deported, forced on a desert march none of them survived."

She continued pointing to figures in the portrait. "Sona, my grandfather's older sister, killed, along with her husband, Ara, and two of their children, Patil and Elnaz, when the Armenians of Van tried to band together and repel the attacks."

Point. "Karekin, the youngest, hid in a well. She starved to death and her corpse was discovered weeks later, but she was considered one of the lucky ones because she didn't die at Turkish hands."

Point. "My great-grandparents, Dikran and Marine, shot in the head at their kitchen table. This is when my grandfather left. He didn't even say goodbye to his parents, the only surviving members of his family, because he didn't think he'd be able to make it out if he did. And they stayed, deluding themselves into believing that things would get better. By 1920, not a single Armenian had been left alive in the town."

Mrs. Khederian's body was rigid as she spoke, the memories forcing her voice tighter. "I know that you're not responsible for any of these things, Nanar. Of course I know that. And I want nothing more than to be able to welcome the girl who gives my Andranik, my firstborn, such joy. But how do I know what your mother's grandparents were doing in 1915? How do I know that your great-grandfather didn't pull the trigger on one of my family members, or that an heirloom of your family's house today wasn't looted from mine one hundred years ago? How can I welcome you into this house when doing so would insult the ghosts of all my ancestors?"

"I don't know, Mrs. Khederian," Nanar answered truthfully.

Nik dropped Nanar's hand, and Alek couldn't decide which of their deflated bodies looked more defeated. Alek's mom walked out to Nanar and put her hand on her shoulder. "Did you drive here today?" she asked kindly.

Nanar nodded her head yes.

"Go home, Nanar, and we'll figure this out in the future, at a time when we're not all so worked up, okay?" Mrs. Khederian instructed her. Nanar nodded yes again and turned, her body slumped in defeat.

"No, it's not okay," Alek said.

"Alek, please," his father interjected gently. "This doesn't concern you."

"I think it does. I think this is a family issue, and this is my family, too, so this concerns me plenty," Alek insisted. "Nanar is a guest here. She was invited by someone in this family into our home, and if there's one thing about being Armenian that I know, it's that you treat guests with respect. So can you explain to me why that doesn't apply now? Are you saying that being anti-Turkish is more important than hospitality in the hierarchy of

Armenian tradition? Because as far as I can see, the genocide happened a hundred years ago, but the Armenian people and their allegedly famous hospitality have been around for approximately three thousand years, so I'm thinking, by nature of seniority alone, hospitality has to trump everything else."

"Alek, you know how hard it is for me to let that boy—"

"His name is Ethan, Dad," Alek said.

"Fine—to let Ethan into this house, knowing he's the reason you lied to us. But we did that. Your mother and I did that. Now let us spend the meal with the two of you. Isn't that enough for us tonight?"

Last week, the idea that Alek's parents would be welcoming Ethan into their home would have been inconceivable to him. When he and Ethan got together, it never occurred to Alek that the relationship was something he'd be able to incorporate into his family life. And suddenly, that doorway was open and the glimmering possibility of being able to have it all beckoned him to step through.

But he couldn't. Not like this. Because it wasn't right.

"You don't get it, do you, Dad? I can't take you up on your offer. And neither would Nik, if our situation was reversed. You of all people should know why. Because you raised us better than that."

"That's my man," Ethan whispered to him.

Alek stepped outside and put his hand on his mother's shoulder. "Our dead ancestors don't care if Nanar has dinner here, Mom."

"How can you know that for sure?" she asked, and Alek could hear how much she wanted him to be right.

"The only thing they want is for us to be happy. And if Nanar makes their great-great-grandson happy—and you'd have to be blind not to see how Nik smiles when Nanar is around—that's all they want. They would want you to choose the living over the dead."

22

TWO HOURS LATER, THE FAMILY KHEDERIAN SAT WITH
Ethan and Nanar in the dining room, drinking Armenian mint
tea and finishing the last scraps of dessert.

"Don't tell me you made the baklava, too," Mrs. Khederian
said, spearing the last bite with her fork and sliding it into her
mouth with relish.

"Of course we did," Alek insisted.

"If by 'made' you mean 'had it delivered from the Damascus
Bakery in Brooklyn,'" Nik amended.

"But you sprinkled the cinnamon and cloves on yourself?" she
asked.

"You got it, Mom," Nik answered proudly.

"You work in the city, right, Mrs. Khederian?" Ethan asked.

"Just south of Port Authority."

"You should check out Market Cafe on 9th Avenue and 38th

Street. One of the best restaurants in New York, in my humble opinion."

"I'm always looking for new places to try." Mrs. Khederian nodded appreciatively.

"And have you been to International Grocery on 40th Street?"

"I've walked by a few times, but I've never had time to go in," she said.

"That place is the bomb—I mean, it's really good," Ethan said. "It's got all these spices; I've never heard of most of them."

"My mom took me there last year," Nanar said. "She said it reminded her of home."

"Nanar, do you mind if I ask you a question?" Mr. Khederian said.

"Of course not."

"How did your mom do it? Conceal her ethnicity, I mean. It can't have been easy."

"She told us she didn't have any other relatives, because she knew they wouldn't play along. Isn't that sad? It turns out I've got an aunt and some cousins I never knew about who live in Baltimore."

"It must be so weird to find out that your past is not what you thought it was," Nik observed.

"It was—I mean, it still is. Because it makes you feel like you're a different person, even though you're not. Especially when you find out that your past is something you've been brought up to hate," Nanar explained. "I'm still working my way through all of that. What happens the next time one of my Armenian friends makes some offhanded Turkish slur?"

"Tell me about it," Ethan commiserated. "You know how many times some bro mistakes me for straight and uses the word *fag*? And then I have to figure out if I'm going to let it slide, which I don't want to do, or correct him and make a big deal out of it, which I also don't want to do."

"That's what makes it hard—there's no clear sense of what the *right* thing is to do," Nanar agreed. "But I knew I had to tell Nik."

"And when I freaked out, did you regret it?" Nik asked.

"I didn't," Nanar replied simply. "I knew I didn't want the burden of carrying the secret. It weighs you down."

"That it does," Alek agreed.

"My mom always said that she believed Turkey's refusal to acknowledge the truth about the genocide hurts Turkey almost as much as it hurts Armenians, because it stops them from having the healing that comes from truth." Nanar took a pause before she continued. "I think that's what made her decision to lie to me all these years even sadder."

"I have something I need to tell everyone," Mr. Khederian blurted, putting down his teacup.

The five other people in the dining room turned to look at him.

"Well, what is it, honey?" his wife prodded.

"I got a job!"

His sons cheered, and his wife put her arms around his shoulders and kissed him on the cheek. "That's wonderful, honey."

"But I turned it down," Mr. Khederian confessed.

Mrs. Khederian retracted her arms. "You did what?"

"Seriously, Dad," Alek asked. "Why'd you bother going on those interviews if you didn't want the job?"

Mr. Khederian spoke carefully, articulating his thoughts for the first time as the words came out of his mouth. "I didn't realize until I actually got one, but I prefer to stay at home. I get to see you guys more than I ever have, and I have some business ideas I've been wanting to get off the ground. Sometimes you need to get what you think you want to realize you never actually wanted it in the first place."

"See, everybody's got something to get off their chest," Ethan said.

"Everyone, that is, except for you, Mom," Alek said.

"I don't know what to say," Mrs. Khederian insisted. "I don't have any secrets, I don't do anything I'm not supposed to, and I have nothing to hide."

"I don't believe it," Alek countered. "There must be something. Something that you think about the moment before you go to sleep with guilt or remorse that rips you up inside."

"Not a thing," Mrs. Khederian said simply.

"Nothing, Mom?" Nik asked.

Mrs. Khederian took the slightest pause before responding. "Well . . ." she trailed off.

"I knew it! I knew it!" Alek said.

"I can't believe I'm admitting this," Mrs. Khederian started.

"Nik was conceived out of wedlock?" Alek asked hopefully.

"Alek has a different father?" Nik guessed, equally hopefully.

Mrs. Khederian looked away, her hand on her throat, agonizing.

Her husband leaned in, intrigued. "Just tell us, honey!" he encouraged.

"Sometimes at Whole Foods I sneak a strand of dill into my package of parsley," she confessed.

For a moment, no one spoke.

"I don't get it," Ethan admitted.

"Well, I don't need an entire container of dill—just one strand for garnish. But I hate the thought of the rest of it going to waste."

"You could freeze it. That's what my mother does," Nanar offered.

"That would work in a soup or stew, but I prefer fresh dill as garnish."

"Let me get this straight," Alek said slowly. "Your big secret is that you steal two cents' worth of dill from Whole Foods every other week?"

"And I feel terrible about it," his mother continued, guilt riddling her face. "After all, it's theft. What if the person at the cash register realized? Or I were captured on one of those video cameras? Can you imagine the scandal?"

"We'd never live it down," Alek deadpanned.

"Well, I don't mean to be rude," Nik said, "but we really should get to bed. Alek and I have a study date early tomorrow."

"For what?" their mom asked. "School doesn't start for another two weeks."

"Well, sure, but when you're taking Honors Algebra II, you've got summer assignments," Alek bragged.

Alek's parents looked at him, joy bubbling in their eyes.

"Don't get too excited—it's just algebra. Ms. Imbrie docked my final paper, so I'll be in Standard English next year," Alek explained.

"This is an outrage!" Mrs. Khederian stood up. "I'm going to talk to Ms. Schmidt first thing Monday morning."

"Mom, chill out. It's fine. It's not like I worked my butt off and earned it. And this'll leave time for other things, like tennis."

"He has a point, Kada." Alek's dad took Alek's mom's hand and she sat back down. "Besides, Honors Algebra is something you can be proud of."

His mother nodded in agreement. "And I'm sure if you work hard, you can make Honors English by junior year, which means you could still be in Advanced by the time—"

"Why don't we take it one year at a time, okay?" Alek said, cutting his mother off.

"What an excellent idea," his mom agreed. "There's no reason to rush anything, is there?" she asked, turning her attention to Nik and Nanar.

Nik, understanding her meaning immediately, put his hand protectively on Nanar's. "What're you saying, Mom? That I should break up with my girlfriend because she's half-Turkish?"

"I'm sure that's not what your mother is saying," Mr. Khederian interrupted. "Just that you want to make sure to go slow so that you have time to digest everything that's happening, like you do after a great big meal. When you're old, like me and your mother—"

"You guys aren't *that* old," Alek interrupted.

"As I was saying, when you get to be older, you see how important it is to let things take their natural course."

"Well, I should be getting home," Nanar said, standing up. "Will I be seeing you at church tomorrow, Mr. and Mrs. Khederian?"

"You and your parents are planning on coming to church this week?" Mrs. Khederian asked, the surprise tingling in her voice.

"Of course. My mother converted before she and my father got engaged. She has as much right to be there as anyone," Nanar insisted.

"We'll see you there," Nik responded. "And I don't know about my parents, but I want you to know that I'll always sit with you, in church or at lunch or anywhere."

Nanar embraced Nik, and then he walked her out to her car. The Khederians turned their attention to Ethan.

"Ethan, you have to understand what an awkward position you've put us in," Mrs. Khederian explained. "You clearly make Alek happy—"

"And he makes me happy," Ethan said.

"Yes, that's clear, too," Mr. Khederian conceded. "But one lovely dinner party isn't actual proof that you're going to be a good influence on our son."

"So what, Dad? I only get to date Ethan if I keep my GPA up above a 3.5?" Alek quipped.

"It isn't that easy, son. I'm afraid we simply can't let—"

"Oh, I don't know, Boghos," Mrs. Khederian interjected.

Alek's dad stopped speaking. He turned and looked at his wife. "We don't disagree in front of the children, remember, Kadarine?" he said in a gentle whisper.

"Well, maybe it's time we started treating them more like adults," Mrs. Khederian continued. "After all, your parents didn't think I was such a good influence on you when we met."

"And why's that, Mom?" Alek asked as neutrally as possible, hoping his tone wasn't betraying how much he wanted the answer.

"I'm three years older than your father, for one thing, which absolutely *scandalized* them. And I was working on my graduate degree, and his mother wanted him to end up with a nice Armenian girl who would stay at home and take care of the house, not some professional, career-minded woman who— how did she put it?" Mrs. Khederian asked her husband. " 'Couldn't roll a proper sarma if her life and her children's lives depended on it.' "

Alek didn't quite succeed in squelching his laughter at imagining his nana talking that way about his mom.

"All right, honey, I think that's enough," Mr. Khederian said.

"Of course, there are certain rules in this household that we expect Alek to follow, Ethan," Mrs. Khederian explained. "And if we don't feel we can trust you to respect those rules, there will be no place for you here. It's that simple."

"I understand." Ethan extended his hand and flashed Alek's mom his most winning smile as they shook on it. Nik returned in time to say goodbye to Ethan, who thanked the Khederians and bid them goodbye.

Alek walked his boyfriend outside. The moment the door closed behind them, Ethan drew Alek into a tight embrace and kissed him fiercely.

"Thank you," Alek murmured.

"For what?"

"For being here."

"Ain't no thing, Polly-O." They kissed until Alek feared his parents would get suspicious, then Ethan unearthed his short-board from the Khederian shrubbery.

"You're going to skate home wearing that suit?"

"The way I feel tonight, I'm basically gonna be flying home," Ethan responded. "Besides, you ever seen me fall?" He kicked off, gliding into the distance. The moment before he disappeared into the night's darkness, he turned around and threw Alek one last kiss.

Alek walked back inside, closing the front door behind him. He leaned against it, relishing the disappearing sensation of Ethan's lips against his own. He gathered himself and rejoined his family in the living room.

His parents were sitting on the sofa, and Nik had begun clearing the dessert dishes.

"I wish the baklava had been a little fresher," Alek said, picking at the leftovers as he helped his brother clean up. "And do you think we undercooked the sarma?"

"Don't do that," his mother scolded him.

"Do what?" he asked.

"That thing of criticizing everything."

Alek looked at her, dumbfounded. "Where do you think I learned it?"

"Well, it's good to have high standards," his father said.

"But it's also good to be able to sit back and enjoy a well-made, home-cooked meal," his mother finished. "That's why food is so important in the Armenian tradition. It takes something you have to do and makes it into something you want to do. Now, you boys sit and your father and I will finish cleaning up."

"You don't have to do that," Nik said.

"We know we don't," his father responded.

"But you two clean when we cook, so it's only fair that we clean when you do the cooking," his mother insisted. "So sit down and relax. You've earned it."

EPILOGUE

"RIGHT AFTER YOU LEFT MY HOUSE, I SKATED OVER TO the ramps. Now, you know how he can be," Becky told Alek, playfully punching Ethan on the shoulder as she told the story. "Especially when he's with the D.A.s."

"It's D.O.s." Ethan struggled to keep up, rolling her giant green suitcase behind him.

"But since I think of you guys as the Dumb-Asses, I call you the D.A.s," she plowed on. "And hurry up. I don't want to miss the train."

"Becky, it's a five-minute walk from your house to the station. We've got plenty of time." Alek readjusted the strap to her overnight bag on his shoulder, wishing for a moment that he had chosen to wear one of his boring old cotton T-shirts instead of the light blue polyester autoworker's short-sleeved button-down he'd picked up at Housing Works. But one of his old T-shirts would've looked terrible with the five-pocket jeans he'd picked for the day. He changed his grip on the smaller suitcase he was rolling, wondering how anyone as little as Becky could possibly pack so much for one week. "The only way you'd miss the train would be if Ethan and I passed out from exhaustion. And can you explain to me why you're not carrying any of your own luggage?"

"Remember when you were straight and a gentleman?" A strap of Becky's trademark overalls hung lazily over her shoulder. "I miss those days. Now, do you want to hear the rest of the story or don't you?"

Alek nodded eagerly, his extra-spiky hair nodding with him.

"So I say, 'Ethan Novick, I have a dinner invitation from Alek Khederian for you,'" Becky continued.

"Everyone cracked up," Ethan added good-naturedly. He was wearing an especially Ethan outfit that day: black, white, and gray camouflage pants and a red sleeveless T-shirt with the words I DO, BUT NOT WITH YOU across the front. "And I was totally embarrassed. But no way I was going to let her off that easy in front of my peeps."

"So he asked me what would happen if he didn't go. So I said, 'I promised I'd get you there, Romeo.' Everyone is dying at this point, they're laughing so hard. So Ethan says he'll skate me for it."

"Why didn't you tell me this is how Becky got you to show up to my house for that dinner party on Saturday?" Alek asked.

"You'll see." Becky's eyes glinted with mischief.

"Now, I don't want to brag," Ethan said, "but I take the course first and I do pretty damn well. Good enough that it's hard for

253

me to imagine one of the guys doing it better, let alone this skinny girl on Rollerblades with frizzy hair who I only know as Polly-O's bestie."

"I spend a few minutes just inspecting the course—you know, judging angles, figuring out momentum, that sort of thing."

"And then *boom*—she's hitting it like a demon possessed," Ethan said. "Jumpin' rails, taking turns, going backward. First time through, she freakin' kills it. No contest. She rolled over and told me that if I didn't show up dressed nice and make a good impression, she'd school me again."

Alek laughed appreciatively, thinking how different Becky's first experience with the D.O.s had been from his own with Jack at the beginning of the summer.

"Well, I have to thank you, Ethan. I don't think my parents realized how important 'this rollerblading thing' was to me until I got home that day and told them about beating you. That's why they decided to send me to skate camp after all."

The three of them reached the train station. "Let's go, boys. Those suitcases aren't going to carry themselves." Ethan and Alek exchanged glances before lugging Becky's suitcases up to the platform.

"It feels so grown-up, taking the train by yourself. You sure you know where you're going?" Alek asked her.

"NJ Trans to Trenton, transfer to the Amtrak, and then down to Wilmington. The camp has a shuttle that'll be picking me up."

"And who's going to help you carry all this shit for the transfer?" Ethan asked.

"I'll be fine, guys, sheesh. Oh, I can barely wait! The first day, they have us do these skill evaluations so they can gauge our levels, you know? Then they tailor-make our curriculum." Becky continued explaining the intricacies and nuances of the skating camp schedule until the train pulled into the station a few minutes later.

"Don't miss me too much," she told Alek.

"Impossible," he shot back.

And then the train whisked her away. Alek and Ethan stood watching it disappear into the distance.

"This summer's been a dream," Ethan murmured.

"I know."

"I just hate that we've only got one week before it ends."

"You've got it all wrong, Eth," Alek said, gently running his hand through Ethan's surfer hair. "This summer's not the dream. We are. You and me. And it doesn't matter what time of year it is, as long as we're together."

"I like that, Polly-O." Ethan smiled.

"We'll wreak havoc, you and me," Alek told him.

"What does that mean?"

"It's a Rufus quote, dumb-ass. It means, Watch out, world: we'll do crazy things together."

"We'll wreak havoc, you and me," Ethan repeated. Alek leaned in to kiss Ethan as the platform vibrated from the force of two express trains shooting through the station, in opposite directions.

STUFFED GRAPE LEAVES

- 1 cup long-grain basmati rice (if omitting lamb, use 2 cups)
- 1 16-ounce jar California grape leaves
- 2 red bell peppers
- 2 onions
- 1 bunch flat parsley, soaked thoroughly in lukewarm water (repeat until the water is clear)
- ¼ teaspoon allspice
- 1 pound ground lamb (optional)
- approximately ¼ cup olive oil (if omitting lamb, make this approximately ½ cup)
- 2 teaspoons salt (or more)
- 1 teaspoon pepper (or more)
- approximately ¼ cup fresh lemon juice (if omitting lamb, make this approximately ½ cup)
- ½ cup tomato paste

1. Cover rice in hot water and let soak while preparing rest of ingredients.

2. Separate and rinse grape leaves under cold running water.

3. De-seed red peppers. In a food processor, pulse red peppers until finely chopped. Put in large mixing bowl.

Pulse onions until finely chopped. Add to peppers in bowl. Remove parsley leaves from stems and pulse in food processor until finely chopped. Add to peppers and onions. Drain rice and add to vegetables in large bowl. Add allspice.

4. Add ground lamb (optional) to vegetable-rice mixture.

5. Add olive oil, salt, pepper, lemon juice. If you're making the vegetarian version, you can taste a little bit of the mixture and adjust the olive oil, lemon juice, salt, and pepper accordingly. If you are making the meat version, just add enough olive oil until the mixture glistens, but not more.

6. Line bottom of pot with a single layer of grape leaves.

7. Lay grape leaves flat on a cutting board, veiny side up. Snip the nub of the leaf with kitchen shears. Place one tablespoon of stuffing in the middle section of each leaf (add a little more for larger leaves, a little less for smaller leaves). Fold in the sides first. They should almost, but not quite, meet. Then flip the bottom of the leaf over the stuffing, and roll up to form a snug (but not too snug) bundle. Place rolled leaf horizontally in the pot, on the outside circumference. The ideal pot is average height with a large circumference (wider than it is tall). Continue laying rolled leaves until the bottom of the pot is filled, then lay

more leaves on top, forming a second, third, and even fourth layer. Continue until all the leaves are rolled, setting aside especially small or torn leaves.

8. Place a few of the small and/or torn grape leaves on top of the rolled ones. Put a plate with a circumference slightly smaller than that of the pot on top of the leaves.

9. Fill a kettle with water and bring to a boil. Let sit for ten minutes. Slowly pour hot water over stuffed grape leaves until the water reaches the bottom of the top-most layer.

10. Bring the water to a boil, drop to a simmer and cook, covered, for 20 minutes. Remove ¼ cup of the simmering water and whisk in the tomato paste until it achieves a sauce-like consistency. Pour evenly over the stuffed grape leaves and continue to cook for another 10 minutes. Remove from heat and let sit for 15 minutes. The grape leaves can be served warm now, or at room temperature.

This recipe is dedicated to my grandmother
Mèline Boghossian (May 29[?], 1915 – February 2, 2010),
a woman with magic in her hands.
—M.B.

ACKNOWLEDGMENTS

Special Thanks:

To Ann E. Imbrie and Wendy Wasserstein, my writer-mentors.

To my friends who read this in various stages and provided invaluable support and insight: Chris Kipiniak, Rosemary Andress, Suzanne Agins, Ariel Whitefoot, and Emily Donahoe. And especially to Sarah Braunstein, my favorite living novelist.

To Emily Jenkins, who provided me with endless and generous guidance throughout this process.

To my dearest un-boyfriend, Andy Goldberg, for introducing me to many wonderful things, among them the music of Rufus Wainwright.

To Taylor Stewart, my consultant for Young Hip Gay Speak.

To my Armenian consultants: Paul Boghossian, Donna Bagdasarian, Aaron Poochigian, and Ara Merjian.

To my agent, Josh Adams, a true gentleman.

And most of all to my editor, Joy Peskin. When other people saw a young theater director, she saw a future novelist. All writers should be lucky enough to encounter a partner so dedicated, intelligent, and valiant. This book would not be if not for her.

• • • • •